ASH

Like a Tattoo

Written by

Dan Waltz

Story, cover art, illustrations, and book layout by Dan Waltz

Assistant Editor: Jan Waltz
Editor: Tony Root

Expanded Edition:
ISBN-13: 978-1522951513
ISBN-10: 1522951512

www.danwaltz.com
www.bullycidal.com

DEDICATION

To all who have felt bullied, one way or another.

ACKNOWLEDGMENTS

First and foremost, I would like to thank my wife, Candis, for all her support she has given over the years. I truly am a lucky man to have a wife who understands and encourages me to follow my dreams. Next, I would like to thank my mother, who has always supported my passions and who has taken on the job as assistant editor. Thanks also to my editor Tony Root. My editors are the reason my stories are enjoyable to read. A big thanks to *Nicholas, Rebecca, and Andrew, for bringing light to some serious issues and overcoming them, which were inspirational to parts of this story, one way or another.

I'd like to thank you, the reader. Your constant support keeps me motivated to keep doing what I do, and to always strive to do it better.

Finally, to nature, which never ceases to amaze and to inspire.

* A special thanks to Nicholas for posing for the cover art.

FITS LIKE A GLOVE
FOREWORD BY MEGAN RENARD

Hello, my name is Megan Renard, and this is my story about my older brother. I should first tell you that I never met him personally, but I do feel that I know him better than anyone he ever knew.

"How?" you ask.

Oh, it's complicated. I'll get to that, but for now, just know I have my ways.

My big brother's name was Ashton, and he was very special. Now, if you're like most people, the minute you heard the word "special," you automatically assumed the "mentally challenged." That wasn't true with Ashton, as he was pretty much a typical kid, on the inside–smart, nice, talented. However, when all was said and done, he did develop some pretty major mental issues that I wish, so badly, that he'd sought help for instead of trying to deal with them himself.

It was on the outside where Ashton had his issues. You see, Ashton was born with a facial deformity called "cleft lip and palate." According to the doctors, it was a pretty severe case and would require a lot of surgeries over a long period of time. "Twenty or more years," they said. It might as well have been a lifetime for a kid who's living in the moment.

His appearance improved with each surgery, a little at a time. Well, except for one time, when Mom and Dad fought for days. Dad felt that Ashton looked a lot worse than he did before the surgery. Mom disagreed at first, but after a while, she finally gave in and jokingly suggested that maybe he has to look worse before he starts looking better. What do I know? I wasn't even born yet, but that kind of made sense to me. After all, whenever I clean my room, it always looks a lot worse before it gets any better.

Mom and Dad kept Ashton home from school until he was eight years old. They were afraid of what people would think, or worse, what they would say after they saw him. They homeschooled him up until then, and I believe it was a good thing that they did. In hindsight, I wish they'd continued.

People can be so cruel. Ashton's first week of public school proved that all too well. He was teased, a lot, and not just for the way he looked either. They made fun of how he talked, as well. Mom called it a speech immm-ped-iment. Sorry, I think I totally botched that word. I just know that it had something to do with the roof of his mouth. He didn't have one, so he had trouble speaking certain words clearly. Okay, that was an understatement. Unless you were around him a lot, my brother could be very difficult to understand. My folks, on the other hand, could understand him just fine, and so could I. I know, I said we never met, and it's true, we never have. Did I mention it was complicated?

Ash, oh I'm sorry, Ashton–I call him Ash for short sometimes. Well, he hid the teasing from Mom and Dad rather well. He hid it for a long time, years actually. He hid it until the teasing became too physical to hide. He still tried, though.

It was Mom who noticed it first, then Dad, after a long period of denial. It seemed Dad always gave Ashton the benefit of the doubt and tried hard to believe all the stories that Ash would bring home. Stories like how he fell one day and skinned his knees, and how he tripped the next day, bruising his arms and cheek. The following week he walked into a door. That one was easy for Dad to believe, since he'd done that himself, but when he did it, it never left a black eye and a big bruise on the opposing side of his body. The accidents started small, but frequent—almost daily. It seemed the larger the accident, the bigger the excuse.

It was the bad limp that Mom really questioned first. It was when Ash fell down a flight stairs at school, or so he claimed. *Fell or was pushed? Just how many times can one fall in a week? He didn't fall that much at home. How clumsy can one be?* The concerns started to build, but it took an unbelievable story of a bookcase falling on him in the library, leaving several bruises and two black eyes, before the first of many school meetings began.

One thing led to another, and soon Ashton was going to school less and less. He started having severe headaches and stomach issues. He became sick a lot, but the funny thing was, he'd always seem to start feeling better shortly after the bus pulled away from the curb. It took a while for Mom and Dad to catch on, but they eventually did.

Soon, my parents became more and more aware, and started looking for things out of the ordinary, like how Ashton's friends, as few as they were, started coming around less and less, and how Ashton's phone seldom rang anymore. They noticed too, just how much alone-time he spent in his bedroom—if not there, out in the backyard. It seemed that all Ashton did anymore was read and draw, which wasn't a bad thing—he loved doing both. His drawings were great—far beyond what a 12-year-old boy should be able to do. Mom and Dad were very proud, but also very concerned.

On one of many trips to the doctor, the doctor noticed how much weight Ashton had lost since his last visit. The doctor asked him if he'd been feeling all right. It took some prodding but Ash finally answered, "I've been feeling drained, lately; tired." Come to find out, bullies had been taking his lunch money at school, and when Ashton brought a lunch, sometimes they would take that too. When they didn't take it from him, they would smash it with their fists. Sometimes they'd throw it hard against the cafeteria wall, then laugh and walk away. Did I mention people could be cruel? I did, didn't I?

As if that wasn't enough, Ashton sometimes would hide a couple pairs of extra underwear in his book bag, in case of emergencies, or should I say, accidents. There were times he was too afraid to use the school bathrooms. He knew once in there, he would be trapped, with no way out. If no one were around to guard the door, he just wouldn't go in. Sometimes the bullies would hide inside and grab you as you walked by. They would drag you in one of the stalls and hold you up by your feet over the toilet bowl. Then they would lower your head down inside, while they flushed it. They called that "a swirly." And if you were dragged into the girls' bathroom, it was called a "girly swirly," a bit more degrading than the standard, I'd guess.

Ashton never went willingly. He always put up a good fight, but it was never enough. The bullies were always bigger, and their thugs always had their backs. Ash would fight hard, kicking and screaming all the way. He would get banged up pretty bad as he struggled to fight back with his head banging hard against the porcelain throne. That explained a lot of the facial bruises and black eyes he would bring home. Mom always wondered where all his underwear was going. She constantly bought him new ones and complained of the washing machine eating them, along with the orphaned socks.

Mom and Dad would make multiple trips to talk to the principal and school officials, but nothing ever seemed to get done. They said they were doing the best they could with the short staff they had, but each still promised to do better as Mom and Dad left their offices.

I just know the bullying never really stopped. It may have slowed at times, but it always returned, and it seemed to be getting more and more dangerous every day.

All Ashton ever wanted to do was to fit in, you know, like a hand in a glove, but he knew deep down it would never happen. Ash was starting to show signs that he'd had enough, and he fought back like he didn't care if he lived or died. The bruises became bigger and the injuries more intense. At times, he would come home so bruised and swollen you could hardly recognize him, yet he still tried to hide it from Mom and Dad.

He eventually became ashamed and too tired to fight back anymore. Every time he did, he just ended up beaten worse than the time before. Ashton was now to the point where he was too afraid to attend school.

One cold day became a day that Mom and Dad would never forget. The school called. It seemed that Ashton never showed up that day, and no one had any idea where he could be. Mom and Dad drove for hours, searching for him. They would return home every now and then, just to see if he had come home, and then they'd return to the streets searching once more. They made a lot of calls and made a lot of stops, but there were no signs of Ash anywhere. Dad wondered if Ash had run away from home.

My parents filed a police report and a statewide Amber Alert was issued. Mom told them everything—all the times he was beaten and bullied at school. The police were appalled that the school would allow such behavior to continue as long as it did. They even offered to check in on him themselves, once they found him. Mom and Dad were grateful for that, but for now, it was freezing cold and getting dark. They needed to find their son, and fast.

On the way back from the police station, something caught Mom's eye. "Stop! Stop the car!" she yelled.

Dad was driving. He normally drove whenever the two went somewhere together. He quickly turned the car into a gas station's parking lot.

"What?" Dad asked.

"Back there, I saw something."

Dad quickly turned the car around and headed back.

"There! Over there, look!" Mom pointed.

"Look at what? I don't see anything."

"On the snow fence, see it?"

"That's his glove!" Nate, our father, said.

A kid's glove was positioned on the fence in a way that it looked as if it was waving to passersby. Dad thought it was a joke at first. Or maybe someone had found it, hoping the owner would see it on the fence and stop by and pick it up. He whipped the car into the parking lot of the school. They both exited the car and bee-lined over to the glove. Dad slid past. The sidewalks were icy. Mom grabbed the glove from the top of the post and examined it. It was Ashton's, all right. His name was written on the inside tag with a magic marker.

A lot of things raced through Mom and Dad's minds at this time, but it all came to a crashing end the moment Mom looked to the ground where she was standing. She gasped for breath and covered her mouth to stifle a scream that never came. She pointed to the ground.

Now Dad saw it too. "That's blood," he spoke under his breath.

He looked around, as did Mom. There were splatters of blood everywhere. The first thing they thought was a possible accident. Maybe a car hit Ash as he crossed the road, but the scuff marks in the snow told a different story. It showed there was a struggle, possibly a fight, or worse, if it could get any worse; maybe an abduction. Now they were worried even more.

They called the police and waited for them to arrive. When they did, they took a lot of pictures, and they also took the glove.

"Evidence," one of the investigators said as he plucked the glove out of Mom's hand and stuffed it into a Ziploc® bag.

Evidence for what, my parents wondered. No one knew

anything, including how Ash's glove got on the fence post in the first place. It was getting dark, and police sent Mom and Dad home. *Maybe he's there,* they hoped, and this time their hopes came true. He was there. Mom found him in his bedroom.

That's when Mom's silent scream surfaced and came out louder than ever. Ashton didn't look good. He was badly bruised, swollen from head to toe and covered with blood.

Dad heard the scream and came running. "ASH!" he yelled as soon as he saw him. He pushed past Mom blocking the doorway and quickly ran to Ash's side. He held him tight.

There was a lot of hugging and crying going on, but I'm not sure that it was all for the good.

Two years later, I was born, and I bet you're still wondering how I know all this if I wasn't around to meet my brother. Well, I would like to tell you that Mom and Dad told me these stories, but they really didn't. The fact is, they went to great lengths to keep them from me. The reason why I know more about my older brother than anyone else gets, well, as I said before, complicated, but I promise you'll understand everything once you finish reading **"Ash, Like a Tattoo."**

This is the end for now, but it's really just the beginning.

Read on for a ride you'll never forget...

CHAPTER 1

A woman in her late thirties sat upon the porcelain throne with her painted-on jeans and hot-pink panties cuffed tightly around her ankles. She'd been feeling quite ill lately. Her last monthly was well over seven weeks ago. Anxiety sank in as her body began to tremble. She sat there, stooped over, not so patiently awaiting the pee-stick for a sign.

"Please no, please no, no, please, no, no dammit, PLEASE, NO!" She was wound up like a spent spring, eventually yelling as the second faint pink line appeared before her watery eyes. "DAMMIT! Why? Why me?!"

A drop of urine teetered back and forth at the end of the stick before dropping between her legs and into the bowl below. She watched on as the droplet created ripples in the water, like growth rings on an old tree, gradually spreading outward. Her body shook as more hot tears began to trail down her rosy cheeks.

First the tears came slowly, one by one, then in pairs, and ultimately, they poured down like rain. When the dark clouds finally departed from her mind, the rain came to an end, and like sunshine, a smile slowly overtook her face. She chuckled out loud.

It was over. For years she didn't want another. Not since the tragedy. Not since the horrifying event that changed her life, as well as the lives of others. She never could fathom the thought of sharing her love with anyone else ever again. Anyone other than the one for whom she grieved for so many years.

The choice had been made, and it was made for her, and she couldn't be happier. Now, like a cool summer rain through a rainbow, different kinds of tears started to fall.

The front door of the house swung wide, crashing hard against the adjacent wall. The spring-loaded rubber stopper designed to absorb the impact had failed weeks ago. It was one of those things that never got replaced, so the door left a nice-sized dimple in the plaster where the doorknob hit. Nathan, her husband of 18 years, came stomping through the threshold.

"SHIT!" Nate yelled, rubbernecking his head around the door to check the damage it left behind. He dropped his briefcase to the floor and kicked it to the wall. He tossed his keys into a wooden bowl centered on the hallway table. After hanging up his coat on the coat tree, he made his way to the kitchen for his daily after-work snack—a 15-year-old routine that he, one day, would miss.

Today was noticeably different though. Today Nate kicked the briefcase up against the wall a little harder than usual, and he didn't really toss his keys into the bowl either, he threw them, just like he did his coat to the coat tree. It wasn't hard to tell that Nate wasn't in the greatest of moods.

"Honey?" Nathan yelled out in a somewhat irritated tone. "I'm home." He grabbed an apple from the fruit bowl centered on the kitchen table. He took one look at it and placed it back in a slightly different location as he walked by, all without missing a stride. He wasn't hungry like he normally was when he came home from work. Something was bothering him in a bad way, but what?

"Honey?!" Nate yelled again, a little louder this time, almost a shout, but he still got the same response. He headed upstairs, skipping every other step, then walked into the bedroom to change out of his stuffy work clothes. Nate never thought, in a million years, that he would ever land a suit-and-tie desk job like he had, and couldn't wait to get home everyday to strip them off. Being more of a jeans and t-shirt kind of guy, he kicked off his shoes and was pulling off his pants, when he noticed light coming from under the door to the master bath.

"There you are." He knocked before turning the handle of the door, then stepped in without hesitation.

There she was, as beautiful as the day they had met.

"Honey?" Her elbows were planted firmly on her knees, body drooped over, with tear-trailed mascara streaming down her face. Nathan instantly forgot about his own problems and feared the worst for hers. "Honey, are you all right? Are you sick?" he asked, kneeling down beside her.

She looked back at him and immediately stood, pulling him up with her. She hugged his neck hard, just about pulling him back to the floor.

"Whoa, honey, what's up? What's wrong?" She didn't answer, nor did she let go. Instead she tightened her grip even harder as more tears made their way down her face. Her feet were stretched to her limits as she reached up and leaned in, hanging on tight so she wouldn't fall. "Honey, honey you're choking me," Nate said, struggling to pry her grip free. "What gives?"

Finally, her grip released one finger at a time as she slowly returned her feet to the floor. She bent down, pulled up her panties, and rolled her jeans up her calves, over her knees, then past her thighs. A couple of light hops later, she was able to zip them up. She handed Nate the pee-stick.

"What's this?" Nate asked, fully aware of what it could be. His eyes widened, then he swallowed hard after seeing the results: two pink lines. Lifting his head, he looked at his wife and did so without breaking into a smile until he saw hers. Right then and there, he knew whatever news he had for her, as important as it was, was not going to be shared at this time.

They both struggled to find the right words to say to

each other. Nathan could see the worry in his wife's eyes. "Are you all right with this?" he finally asked in a soothing voice. She shook her head, burying her face into his chest. "It will be all right," Nate assured her, grasping for some reassurance himself.

•••

CHAPTER 2

Worried, Nate hardly slept a wink and knew that his wife, Brandy, didn't sleep much either. He had lain there all night watching her breathe as she tossed and turned, while his own mind raced to and fro. He was in desperate need to find a solution to the problems at hand. Solutions were hard to come by, and comforting Brandy while she slept served only to temporarily occupy Nate's weary mind.

Nathan stroked Brandy's hair, trying to calm her body as it twitched and churned, reacting to those crazy nightmares she'd always had, ever since their first child's death. It wasn't until 5:15 a.m. when her body finally came to rest long enough to enter a peaceful REM sleep. She needed the rest. She didn't have to get up until 10 a.m., plenty of time to make her doctor's appointment at noon to get checked out. They both wanted confirmation of the results they'd gotten from the pee-stick before it became official and they announced the news to anyone. Those pee-sticks have been

17

known to be wrong in the past. Considering his current situation, in the back of his mind Nate wished it would be wrong this time.

Nate rolled his little, white ass out of bed bright and early that morning, just like he did any other day before work. The only difference this time was that he did it without the use of an alarm clock and without turning on the lights. He got dressed under the clock's digital glow, carefully opening and closing dresser drawers, ensuring little to no noise was heard as he felt around for his clothes. His only hope was that his socks and shirt were right-side out when he put them on. Having the clothes match was just an added bonus that he wasn't too concerned about. Where he was going it didn't really matter.

Nathan did his best not to awaken his beautiful bride from the much needed deep sleep she was finally getting. She laid so innocently on her back with a pool of drool in the right corner of her mouth, awaiting that right moment to shoelace its way down and puddle on her pillow. She snored lightly.

Sticking to his daily routine, Nate grabbed his coat, keys, and briefcase before leaving the house just before sunrise, quietly closing the door behind him.

Normally, Nate would be going to work at this time of day, but that wasn't the case today. He had a few errands to run, making a quick detour left where he normally would have taken a right to go to his office. He drove for a few miles before stopping at the state park where he would sit and feed the pigeons, trying to clear his troubled mind.

The morning was absolutely beautiful. Ducks and geese flew in two by two, as they blindly made their landings in a low formation, disappearing right before Nate's eyes into the low-lying fog. The fog was thick, causing Nate to wonder how many times the birds had to practice their landing to have such blind faith.

When the fog finally lifted from the pond, it revealed hundreds, if not thousands, of waterfowl. Nathan could hear them but never imagined there were so many until the fog had completely dissipated. He was in awe. It was now 9:15 a.m. when he took in the beautiful sight.

After an hour of sitting and feeding the pigeons, Nate watched the sun as it rose over the tree line. It was a cool morning, and he welcomed the warm rays upon his face and hands. He poured the last cup of coffee from his thermos and slurped a few sips before pulling the newspaper from his coat pocket. He began to read the daily news.

The headlines that Nate read were quite disturbing, to say the least, and the stories that followed them were even worse.

"SOMALI PIRATES KIDNAP ANOTHER AMERICAN FROM A FREIGHTER OFF THE COAST OF AFRICA." *Seems that happens all too often.* Nate thought.

Another read, "THE CDC PREDICTS

THOUSANDS TO DIE IN THIS YEAR'S STRAIN OF INFLUENZA." *Another overly exaggerated yearly event, designed to sell the public more drugs.*

"ICEBERGS MELTING AT AN ACCELERATED PACE, GLOBAL WARMING BLAMED BY MILLIONS." *If there is such a thing.*

"JAPAN'S RADIATION LEVELS EXCEED SAFETY LIMITS, EVACUATION IMMINENT." *Wow, what's next, California?*

"MELTING STARFISH WASH UP ON CALIFORNIA SHORES." *Damn, I hate it when I'm right.*

"AN ISLAND OF CONTAMINATED TRASH THE SIZE OF TEXAS MAKES ITS WAY ACROSS THE PACIFIC FROM FUKUSHIMA, JAPAN, AND IS EXPECTED TO SLAM THE CALIFORNIA COASTLINE IN THE NEXT FEW DAYS." *Hmmmm, that explains the melting starfish.*

Nathan turned the page only to read more depressing news. The paper was full of it. He started reading the next headline when his phone rang, interrupting his train of thought. A photo of his wife appeared on the screen of his iPhone. "Hello?" he answered.

"Hi, hon, it's me."

"Brandy? Hi, what's up, everything okay?" Ducks and geese quacked and honked loudly in the background.

"I'm fine, Nate. Was that geese I hear? Where are you?" she asked.

"Oh, it's just the TV. I'm walking through the lobby headed to a meeting with the web group. Some nature channel, I guess. So, what's the good news?"

"You're going to be a dad again, Nate." Silence filled Brandy's earpiece. It took a few seconds to absorb, but Brandy finally realized what she had said. "Oh my gosh, I'm so sorry, Nate. I didn't mean 'again.' Once a dad, always a dad, right Nate?" She paused, "Nate?"

Brandy was clueless of the real reason for Nate's hesitation.

"That's all right, hon, not a big deal."

"It is a big deal. I'm such a......"

"No, no you're not, you are beautiful and you're having my baby and that's all that matters," Nate interrupted.

"*We* are having a baby, Nate. We."

Nate just shook his head, drifting back into deep thought. "I have to go, dear. I'm walking into the meeting right now, and they're all staring at me on my phone. I'll see you when I get home. I love you."

"Make lots of money; we're going to need it! Love you too!"

Wow, she didn't need to say that, Nate thought as he hung up the phone. "Lots of money. What a joke. It takes a job to do that," he said aloud. "What am I doing anyway? I don't deserve her. Look at me, 40 years old, premature balding, a beer belly to boot, and I don't even drink beer.

And now jobless, to top it all off." Nate paused to take the last sip of coffee from his cup. He lifted the thermos and shook it, then slammed it down hard against the park bench. Empty. "What is a gorgeous girl like her doing with a shmuck like me, anyway?" he wondered. "It breaks all the rules. Nines date nines and tens; tens don't marry sixes. Shit, who am I kidding, I'm probably only a five." He went back to reading more of the depressing paper.

"SCHOOL BULLYING AT AN ALL TIME HIGH" was the next headline he read, but he chose not to read any further. The subject hit way too close to home for him. He didn't need another reminder of the worst day of his life. Not now. He was depressed enough already. Nate quickly turned to the sports section of the paper where he was greeted with more depressing news. "DETROIT TIGERS LOSE THE ALCS. THE CARDINALS ARE GOING TO THE WORLD SERIES."

"That's it! I've had enough. My problems are nothing compared to everything going on around us. I can fix this, dammit! I'll find another job before she ever finds out that I lost this one. I can do this," he ranted out loud.

That's all it took to light Nate's fire, but it didn't prove that easy. Nothing's ever that easy. Day after day, the state park became Nathan's new office. He even packed lunches and kept a small cooler in the trunk of his car. When it rained, he stayed in the car or spent time at the local diner down the road. He would look for jobs in the newspaper, fill out applications at local businesses, and drop off his resume wherever he could, wherever they'd accept it.

It seemed hopeless. Nate was out of resources and was about to resort to drastic measures: Craigslist. He tried thinking of odd jobs he could do; *a handyman,* he thought, then shot himself down thinking of all the odd jobs around the house that he's neglected over the years.

This went on for days, and the days quickly turned to weeks. It seemed that there were no jobs in the cards for Nathan.

Nate continued to fill out more applications and hand deliver more resumes, even for jobs in fields he knew nothing about. He was desperate and started thinking that flipping burgers was in his future. A job was a job after all, especially when there was a baby on the way.

Two weeks had passed with only two phone calls for interviews, one of which he was over-qualified for, while the other, the complete opposite. That particular interview was with the city. Nevertheless, Nate felt that the interview went well, and he had high hopes. He thought that he and the interviewer, the mayor himself, really hit it off, and Nathan kind of felt he had a chance. He waited for days, and still his phone never rang.

Now into week three, the only time his phone ever rang was when Brandy called. She mainly called to have Nate pick something up on his way home from work. Dinner one day, a loaf of bread and a gallon of milk the next. Pretty soon it would be for diapers and formula. Nate would have to find a way to get those items with no money.

Desperate thoughts of crime soon entered Nathan's mind. He visualized himself shoplifting and running from the police. His daydreams soon turned to daymares, as he saw himself panhandling on the streets, picking up cans out of ditches, and even dumpster diving. Depression settled its way in.

Nate didn't know what to do. Panic ran through his veins time and time again, like a heart attack waiting to happen. More than once he was convinced he was having one. He had a baby on the way and he was jobless. To make things worse, he had been lying to his wife for the past three weeks about what he'd been doing with his time.

Stress was surely taking a toll and at a very rapid pace. Nate's blood pressure rose and he had already gone through two bottles of Advil, just to keep his headaches under control.

Brandy would be wondering why he didn't bring a paycheck home this Thursday, and then he would have no other choice but to come clean and tell her. *It's not going to go well.*

Thursday afternoon came quickly, and Nathan had given up hope. The fat lady was singing the last chorus on the radio, and the moment of truth awaited him. He put his car in drive and headed for home. Tonight was the night he was going to spill the beans and tell Brandy the truth. And beg for her forgiveness.

Nathan turned out of the park in haste, only to be greeted by a series of car horns going off all at once. He swerved off the road to avoid an oncoming truck he'd just cut off. Nate's mind was not on his driving. Shaken, he carefully crept back onto the blacktop and slowly accelerated for home.

Like an actor on his way to a set, Nate rehearsed every line of what he was going to say to her. He went over it again and again on his way home. On the straightaways, he even watched himself in the rearview mirror. "I look like a moron," he said. The more he rehearsed, the more unnatural it sounded, and he thought his facial expressions were just ridiculous. *I'm screwed,* he thought. "DAMMIT! Why, why did this happen to me?" He slapped the steering wheel hard with the palm of his hand.

Nate didn't realize just how slowly he was driving as cars lined up behind him. One by one, they would pass, some laying on their horns in disgust; more even shared nice hand gestures as they passed by.

"Assholes," Nate said as he took a deep breath while negotiating his last turn. Just two more miles and he would be home. He began to sweat as he rehearsed his lines one last time. Just three words into his speech, his phone rang. "Not today," he whispered, just knowing it was Brandy wanting him to stop at the store on the way home. Maybe she wanted pizza, or maybe just a fountain drink. She had a thing for fountain drinks, but Nate's mind was set. He wasn't stopping anywhere for anything and avoided the call.

The phone kept ringing. *Maybe it's important. She'd never let it ring that long. Maybe an emergency?* He gave in and looked down at the phone. The phone read, "private." It wasn't Brandy after all. He normally didn't answer private calls, but the persistent ring told him that he'd better. *Life couldn't get any worse.* He answered right before it went to voicemail. "Hello, this is Nathan."

"Nate?"

"Yes. Who is this?"

"This is the mayor from the city office. We had an interview together last week, do you remember?"

"Stan? Yes, of course. What can I do for you?"

"Is this a good time, Nate?"

"As good as any," Nate replied, looking up his driveway as he passed by.

"Well, Nate, I would like to offer you the job. If you're still available, that is."

Nate's body started to shake uncontrollably, and he found it difficult to drive, hold the phone, and talk at the same time. He pulled the car to the side of the road and cleared his throat.

"Nate? Are you there?"

"Yes, Stan, I'm here. Sorry, I had to find a place to pull over. I was driving. You have no idea what this phone call means to me, Stan. And, yes, the answer's yes. I'm available, and I'll take it."

"I haven't even told you what it is yet, Nate."

"It doesn't matter, Stan. When can I start?"

"Give your employer two weeks, then report here at 8 a.m. sharp the day after. How does that sound for you?"

"I don't have anyone to give two weeks' notice to, Stan. They closed the doors three weeks ago. May I start tomorrow?"

"Tomorrow's Friday, Nate. How about Monday?"

"Monday it is. Thanks, Stan. Thank you so much."

Nate hung up the phone and tried hard to hold back his emotions but failed. He cried like the newborn baby he was about to have. After a few minutes, he pulled himself together and drove down the street to the florist. He took the last $45 from his wallet and bought roses for his wife, something that he hadn't done in years. He figured it would be a good investment since he had a lot of sucking up to do.

Nate pulled in his driveway, parked the car, and took in a deep breath. "Okay, here goes nothing," he said as he slowly exhaled, stepping out of the car.

"What is this?" Brandy asked after smelling the roses she was just handed.

"They're for you."

"Thank you, but why? What's the occas....did you wreck the car, Nate? You haven't bought me roses in years. What did you do?"

"The car is fine. It's just because everything is going to

be all right, that's all, and that I love you."

"Aw, thanks, dear. You're the best." Brandy looked around for a vase but realized they didn't have one. Nate improvised by cutting the top off a two-liter and filling it with water.

"No, no I'm not. I'm a shmuck," he finally replied.

"A shmuck? What are you talking about, Nate?" Brandy asked with a confused look.

"I owe you an apology, or two, or ten, maybe even twenty."

Brandy's confused look turned into a worried one. She quickly thought the worst. "Nate, what have you done?" She paused only for a second. "It's the secretary isn't it? Her and her cute little ass? Damn you, Nate! I knew there was something."

"Honey, no, no, no, no, no, that's not it. It's not what you think."

"Oh, then what? What have you done?"

"I've been lying to you for the past three weeks, and I'm trying to come clean and tell you how sorry I am, if you'll just give me a chance." The flowers dropped to Brandy's side. "Do you remember the day I found you in the bathroom? The day you showed me the pregnancy test that first time?"

"Yeah, what's this all about, Nate?" she impatiently asked, gritting her teeth.

"Well, I had a bit of bad news to tell you that day, but

then I found out you were going to have a baby, so I couldn't tell you. I didn't want to spoil the moment."

"Nate, that was three weeks ago!"

"I know."

"Well, are you going to tell me now?" she asked.

Nate shook his head. "You see, hon, I lost my job that day. They closed the doors, and I've been out of work ever since."

"WHAT! You've been gone every day. Where have you been?"

"Down at the park mostly, feeding the pigeons and ducks, you know, like you see on TV. Then I started intently looking for a job, after my depression and self pity wore off. I'm really sorry, dear, I couldn't bring myself to tell you. Not after your great news. You had enough on your mind. Please forgive me."

"You should have told me!" Pissed, Brandy grabbed the flowers out of the makeshift vase and threw them onto the couch, spraying water everywhere. "You shouldn't have gone through that alone. You're always there for me. Just once, just once, Nate, I would like to have been there for you. You, youuuu aaaaASS! GRRRRRRR," she growled and stomped off into the kitchen.

Nathan stared at the flowers scattered across the couch and inhaled a deep breath. *Well, that went well. Follow her, you fool,* he thought to himself. He picked up the flowers and placed them back in the vase, leaving a few stragglers behind.

He then tracked Brandy down in the kitchen. "Hon, I'm sorry, but please know, I couldn't tell you. I didn't know how, and besides, it all worked out. I got a new job today. I start Monday."

"Yeah, doing what?" she asked through teary eyes.

"I," Nate paused. "Well, I don't really know. Something for the city. It's a government job. It has to be good, right?"

"You accepted a job, and you don't even know what it is?"

"It didn't really matter. There's a baby on the way, and I need a job, so I took it. I guess I'll find out what it is Monday morning."

Nate smiled. It was an infectious smile, at that. Brandy didn't want to, but she couldn't help but to smile back. She knew she was lucky to have him. She beat his chest with her fists.

"I love you, you frickin' jerk," she said.

"Jerk? You can do better than that."

•••

CHAPTER 3

Nearly nine months went by. Nathan still had his job with the city, and he loved it. At home, he had just finished turning one of the bedrooms into a nursery when Brandy appeared in the doorway, holding her protruding belly.

"It's time," she said.

Nate's eyes opened wide. "Really?" Brandy nodded. "Okay, well..." It was like eight months of preparation just flew out the window, and for the life of him, he couldn't remember what to do. Nate looked back and forth, knowing he should be grabbing something but couldn't remember what. His brain turned to oatmeal.

"The go-bag?" offered Brandy in a calm voice.

"Right! Right, the go-bag, grab the go-bag! No wait, I'll grab it, you do nothing. I've got this." Nate just stood there thinking, *Where?*

"Bedroom closet, Nate," Brandy answered, practically reading his mind.

"The closet. Of course. What would I do without you?" Nate turned to the hall and ran to the bedroom, skidding around the corner. He grabbed the bag and ran back to the nursery, only Brandy was no longer there.

Nate ran down the stairs. "There you are." Brandy was standing next to the front door, coat and purse in hand. "You're ready?" She nodded. "Good. Let's go." Nate ran out the door and down the sidewalk. He stopped when he realized that Brandy wasn't with him. "Shit!" He backtracked to the door and opened it to find Brandy standing on the other side, arms folded. "I'm so sorry, Brandy."

"Nate, relax. There's time."

Less than an hour later, Brandy nervously lay on a hospital bed with her feet up in stirrups. Her husband stood behind her, rubbing her neck and shoulders, and coaching her the best he remembered how. He wished now that he had made it to those Lamaze classes, instead of all those late nights at the office.

Overcome by feelings and a little deja vu, Brandy felt exhausted. Her sleep had been interrupted by uncontrollable contractions for the past eleven hours. It seemed that this child of theirs would never arrive.

"Breathe, dear. You have to breathe." Nathan demonstrated a fast, repetitive breath and urged Brandy to do the same, as he held a cold cloth to her forehead.

"Just one more time, Brandy. I can see the head," the doctor said, his voice slightly muffled behind a white mask. "Okay, this is it, but you have to push, and push hard."

Brandy drew in a deep breath and with every ounce of

energy she could muster, she pushed. Every vein and muscle in her neck bulged to their limits. She cried out in pain until she could push no longer. She fell back silently against the slope of the bed, her chest heaved, and she panted like an overheated dog. Her arms dropped to her sides. She was spent and had nothing more to give.

Seconds later, a baby's cry broke the silence.

"Congratulations, you two. It's a girl," came a deep voice from behind the sheeted curtain, supported only by Brandy's knees. After clearing the baby's airway, the doctor handed the baby over to the nurse, who, in turn, cleaned the baby and wrapped her up tightly, like a little present. *No complications this time*, the doctor thought as he counted silently to himself—*ten fingers, ten toes, full lips, and palate*. The doctor sighed.

Brandy leaned over to look around her legs. Her eyes met the doctor's with grave concern. It was the same doctor who delivered their first child.

"No worries this time, Brandy," he said, not needing to know what she was questioning.

Brandy exhaled a long sigh of relief before finding her second wind. She was ready to hold her bundle of joy, a healthy baby girl with no deformities, unlike her first. She patiently waited.

Nathan and Brandy's firstborn had been born with a cleft lip and palate. The poor boy's face showed extremely abnormal facial deformities, and, as a youth, he was heavily teased for his appearance, as well as the speech impediment accompanying his condition. He was teased his entire life, as short as it was. The countless surgeries that he endured helped tremendously over time but did nothing for the mental and physical scarring left behind.

The boy was teased and bullied so relentlessly that it eventually led him to his own demise. After enduring a lifetime's worth of ridicule in just a few years spent in public school, he'd finally had enough. At the very young age of twelve, the boy took his own life.

"Split-lip" was the most common name bullies called him, but there were many others.

"Baby talk, baby talk, it's a wonder you can..." Even though it was an old saying, it still hurt deep inside.

"Hey kid, split the shit out of your lips. I can't understand what you are saying." The kids, his peers, were very cruel.

"Don't give me no lip" was as common as "hello" to him.

"Bite your lip, Ashton. Oh, it looks like you already have." It went on and on, an endless barrage of insults and pain.

The boy's name was Ashton, and he was quite the artist. His love for nature showed in all of his drawings, but unfortunately he was teased for that as well. "What do you call an artist with no 'palette?' Ashton, of course." They all would laugh, most unaware of what it was doing to him on the inside.

While at school and even on the bus rides to and fro, those hurtful sayings were recited to him over and over again, until they were permanently drilled into his head. There was hardly a day when he didn't hear them, and when there was, he still heard them in his own mind, echoing in his head until he started believing them himself.

Ashton became bitter. Aggression took control for a while. He let it build and build, until he finally exploded. The fights were heartbreaking, and he would end up beaten beyond recognition at times, and the school did little to nothing about them.

One day, Ashton, shortly before his death, painted on his bedroom wall, *That which does not kill us makes us stronger,* a quote by Friedrich Nietzsche. This became one of his favorite quotes and one he lived by, as he would never back down from a fight, nor would he ever reveal his tormentors. He knew the consequences if he did: an even worse beating, if that were possible. He knew he was to grow up strong, or not grow up at all.

Ashton was strong in public because he had to be, but deep down inside, he was weak, just a meek little boy with a broken heart and hurt feelings.

Brandy was flabbergasted by the uncaring responses she got every time she made the school aware of what was going on. She reported every bloody nose and every black eye, but she always got the same type of response. "What do you expect, Mrs. Renard? Kids will be kids, after all." Everywhere she turned, they just shook their heads. "Sorry, we're dong our best." Or, "We'll try to keep a better eye on him."

"Try," they said, but not hard enough.

Eventually, the boy had endured all he could take. If this

was the way life was going to be, then he wanted no part of it. The very persons who vowed to keep him safe while away from home had failed to protect him. He now was too scared to go to school.

One day Ashton climbed up on his bunk bed and removed a ceiling tile from above. He wrapped a rope around a rafter and tied the other end around his neck. He didn't even make a noose. He tried, but he didn't know how. Instead, he just tied a knot, a double knot at that, and he tied it much too tight. The boy instantly couldn't breathe. He choked and gasped for air as he clawed at his neck, trying to loosen the knots, but to no avail. Everything he tried just made the knots even tighter.

Ashton would have no time to finish the note that he'd started. The note was for his mom and dad to tell them that this was no fault of theirs, and that he loved them. The knots were simply too tight, and he couldn't see what he was doing. His face turned red with panic. The redness quickly turned blue, then faded to pale white as he ran out of air to breathe. He couldn't even collect enough air in his lungs to let out a scream for help.

When he ran out of air, his body slumped forward, hitting his eye hard on the bedpost before tumbling off the side of the top bunk of the bed. Before his feet could hit the floor, the rope pulled taught against the rafters and his head snapped back firmly. He had hanged himself.

A note pad was found on the floor next to the bed, with nothing written on it, but...

Dear Mom and Dad.

Please forgive me. I...

That was ten years ago.

This is now...

CHAPTER 4

"Just look at her, Nate. Watch her play." Brandy and Nate stood in front of the kitchen sink. They peered through the small window together into their backyard, Megan's playground. They watched as their seven-year old child played around a large tree, just off the side of the deck.

"She sure has grown fast, hasn't she?" Brandy said.

"Where has the time gone?" Nate asked, wrapping his arms tightly around Brandy's waist from behind. Their bodies melted together as one, as they swayed to the music playing in their own heads. "So, what do you think she's doing?"

"Well, it looks like she's going to rake the yard," Brandy answered.

"Wow, now that's cool. I hope she does the front yard too," said Nate.

"You might be pushing it there."

"Yeah, you're probably right." He paused. "Listen, I have

to run. I'm late already. I have a couple of inspections that need to be done before noon. See you in a few hours." Nate bent down and kissed Brandy on the neck behind her ear, instantly sending chills up her spine.

"Any more of that and you're not going anywhere, fella," she said as she cinched the robe she was wearing a little tighter around her waist, choking the chills out. She sighed as she watched her husband walk out of the room. Then she turned to watch her little girl play a little longer. Life was good.

But life wasn't always good for Nate and Brandy. No, there was a time when life was a living hell for the both of them.

Brandy poured herself a cup of coffee then pulled a small framed photo down from the top shelf of the bookcase. She shouldered up against the archway to the great room and stared long and hard at the photo as she drifted off to another place and time. As she reminisced, it wasn't long before tears filled the corners of her eyes. One by one those tears released and rolled off her slippery cheeks and splashed onto the hardwood floor. She swiped the tears away with the back of her hand, then mouthed the words, "I miss you, Ashton," before returning the photo high, out of reach and out of sight, where a little girl would never notice it.

More tears streamed down Brandy's face as she wondered when, if ever, the right time would be to tell Megan about her deceased big brother, and maybe the troubles he went through. "She's not old enough to understand yet," she kept telling herself, as she continued to watch through the glass sliding door while her daughter played outside. She sat and finished her coffee, all the while wondering if sheltering Megan from reality was the right thing to do. Three cups of coffee and a danish later, she finally got up to do the dishes and, once again, watched Megan through the small window above the sink.

After the dishes were done, Brandy decided to clean the sliding door after noticing just how disgustingly dirty it was. While cleaning the door, she overheard Megan talking to someone, as if that someone were standing right next to her, but there was no one around. She cleaned a little slower to listen in on the conversation.

There was nothing strange about the conversation at first, a typical child talking to an imaginary friend. All kids have them, especially at Megan's age, but eventually the conversation became weird to Brandy, so she listened more intently. It was like listening to a one-sided phone conversation between two adults. She stopped cleaning, as the squeakiness of the glass covered some of Megan's words. She swore she heard Megan mention Ashton's name more than once in the conversation. She listened on, and again the name was mentioned. She was sure of it this time, but she couldn't recall ever using the boy's name in front of Megan. *She couldn't know. Could she?*

"Hey Meg, who were you talking to over there?" Brandy asked when Megan finally came up to the door.

"Just a friend," she answered.

"Does your friend have a name?"

"Yes, silly, everyone has a name," Megan replied, seemingly avoiding the question. She walked into the house and slid the door closed behind her, cutting the conversation short.

Brandy didn't follow. She had hoped her daughter volunteer a better response, but Megan didn't cooperate. *Baby steps, Brandy, don't pry,* she thought to herself.

Once Megan was inside and out of sight, Brandy made her way over to the tree where Megan was had been having her conversation. She looked up, down, and all around, but all she saw was the cement garden gnome standing at the base of the tree next to a tiny wooden door. "Was she talking to you?" Brandy asked aloud, not really expecting an answer. She looked around the tree again, finding not even a bird in sight.

"Hi dear," said Nate, startling Brandy as he appeared around the corner of the house.

"Oh! Nate, you scared me half to death. I didn't hear you."

"Sorry, you must have been deep in thought. What were you looking for?"

"Oh, nothing."

Nate thought it was a strange reply. He clearly saw her looking for something, but he shrugged it off. "Okay. Well then, what's for dinner? I'm starved." It was Nate's turn to look around the yard. "Figures. Just what I thought."

"What's that, dear?"

"She was playing with the rake earlier, wasn't she? She only raked under the tree."

"Oh yeah, I noticed that too. Isn't that funny?"

Nate nodded and not so patiently awaited a response to the dinner question. "Dinner?" he asked again.

"I'm sorry, Nate. I had nothing planned. How about we order pizza and maybe watch a movie? Any objections?"

"Sounds good to me, dear." He paused and checked Brandy out as if they were meeting for the first time. "Are you all right?"

"Yeah, fine. Why?"

"You seem, you know, off. Something happen today?"

"I just have a lot on my mind, that's all." Brandy paused a moment, then no matter how hard she tried to hold it back, she spilled the beans. "She doesn't have any friends, Nate. None. No one calls. No one comes over. She plays all by herself, all day long, every day, and talks to her imaginary friends. I overheard an entire conversation she had with a garden gnome, Nate! A garden gnome! Don't other kids like her? It's not right and seems very unhealthy. She needs to socialize."

"Hey, hey, hey, what's this all about? She has friends. She has..." Nate paused to think, but came up blank.

"Exactly, you don't know of any either. A girl her age should have plenty of friends. She should be having sleepovers, tea and pajama parties, but she doesn't. She doesn't have any of that. Megan has never showed any signs of wanting any friends, and I don't know what to do?"

"Maybe we should talk to her school counselor. Let's get her involved in some after-school activities and socialize."

"But, what if..."

"No! No 'buts' or 'what ifs.' It won't happen to her, so don't even think about it."

"But…"

"Brandy. No buts. What happened to Ashton will not happen to Megan. End of story."

"Well, okay," Brandy answered. "I'll go see the counselor tomorrow." She paused. "Oh, and Nate, have you ever mentioned Ashton to Megan?"

"No, never. Why?"

"I overheard her conversation while she was playing today, and I heard her mention his name."

"Oh yeah? Who was she talking to? I thought she didn't have any friends."

"I don't know who she was talking to. There was no one else there. I assume just her imaginary friend, maybe the garden gnome."

"All right, well, what did you hear?"

"I thought I heard her mention Ashton's name a couple

of times."

"Oh, well, I haven't said a word about him, dear."

"Me either, but how else could she know?"

"Well, I don't know. Are you sure that's what you heard?"

"I'm pretty sure, Nate. I heard it more than once. Maybe it's time?"

"Oh, I don't know, hon."

"We could at least talk about it."

"We'll do that, real soon, I promise. Now, how about that pizza and movie? I'm starved."

"We just had pizza two nights ago. Are you sure you want it again?"

"You know I could eat it every day."

Brandy nodded with a smile as Nate walked into the house to get changed. She then turned to the tree and daydreamed a conversation with herself. *Nate and I used to go out and talk to the tree a lot. I haven't done it for a long time, but I used to. We used to.* She paused. Then her mind argued back. *That's different, Brandy. We were mourning Ashton. It's like when people go to visit their loved ones' gravesites. They sit and talk to them, as if their loved ones were right there with them. People know that they aren't there, but they still do it anyway. It makes them feel better.*

•••

CHAPTER 5

Monday morning, Brandy drove Megan to school. Meg usually rode the bus, but Brandy wanted to talk to the school counselor about her daughter's social issues, so she offered her a ride. There was a boy on the bus who constantly gave Megan a hard time, so she gladly accepted any ride when offered.

When they arrived at school, Megan headed one way while Brandy walked towards the office. "See you after school, Megan. I love you," she said.

"Mommmm... Love you too," Megan meekly replied over her shoulder as she continued walking to her classroom.

The door to the counselor's office was open, but Brandy knocked on the doorjamb anyway before entering.

"Please come in. The door's always open," called a voice from across the room. "Please, have a seat." A silhouetted figure appeared behind a desk as Brandy entered.

"Thank you." Brandy tucked her short skirt around her legs and sat down on the cold leather chair. Chilled, she folded her arms and crossed her legs, which became nothing but a distraction to the counselor.

"Well," the counselor, a well-dressed older man with a comb-over, said while walking towards her and away from the bright window. He looked over his spectacles at Brandy. "What brings you in today?" he said, struggling to hold eye contact.

"It's my daughter, Megan."

"Megan, Meghannnnn? Hmmm."

"Renard. Megan Renard," Brandy offered.

"Ah yes, Renard. Megan's a nice girl. Quiet. She never really gets into any trouble, does she?" He paused, clearing his throat. "I'm sorry, I'm afraid I don't know a lot about the good ones. And you are, Miss?"

"Mrs. Renard."

"Oh, of course. Well, I'm very pleased to meet you, Mrs. Renard."

"Please, Brandy." She shifted in her chair, noticing that the counselor's eyes caught every movement. She smirked, soaking up the attention.

"Very well. As I was saying, Brandy, it goes with the job. I know all the bad ones quite well."

"Oh, I'm sure you do." Brandy smoothed her skirt around her legs, toying with his thoughts.

"What brings you here this morning?" he asked again.

"It's Megan," she paused. "Well, she practically has no friends, no social life at all, nor does she do anything after school." She paused again, noticing the counselor's wandering eyes. She adjusted her skirt some more. "My *husband*," she emphasized, "and I were just wondering what programs, if any, were available to her."

The counselor turned around like a wounded puppy with his tail tucked between his legs. "Well, what does she like to do?" he grumbled. "Run? Play basketball? Baseball? How about cheerleading?"

"I'm afraid she hates all sports, actually." Brandy purposely repositioned her legs one more time, just to see if she was imagining things or if he actually was the dirty old man he seemed to be.

The counselor cleared his throat again, and then stuttered, "W-w-we have a great debate club. Or, how about chess? Does she read? Choir? Does-s-s-s she enjoy singing?"

Brandy chuckled, knowing the answer to her question. "Yes, she loves to read and sing. She's constantly humming one song or another."

"Allllll right, very well, choir meets Tuesdays and Thursdays after school in Room 312. Have her report there tomorrow. I'll let the teacher know, so she can be expecting her."

"Perfect! Thank you so much, Mr. ...?"

"Oh, I'm sorry, where are my manners?"

Certainly not here, Brandy thought.

"Mr. Babcock, and you're very welcome, Mrs. Brandy—Renard," he corrected himself. "I sincerely hope this does the trick for you."

"Yes, me too, and thanks again for your time."

"The pleasure was all mine." He took her hand, helping her out of her chair, and then started to lift her hand up to his lips for a kiss.

Brandy nodded and pulled her hand back, seeing herself to the door, but not without a very strong vibe that the counselor was staring at her ass as she walked away. Her intuition was, of course, correct.

Mrsss. Renard, mmm mmm, the counselor thought with his eyes as they followed her behind, all the way out the door and down the hallway.

Not that the counselor was much different than any other men; Brandy was a very attractive woman, and she frequently had the feeling of being watched. At her age, she'd take all the flattery she could get.

•••

CHAPTER 6

Three weeks of choir had passed, and all seemed well, until the phone rang one day.

Brandy picked up the phone. "Mrs. Renard?" The voice on the other end stifled Brandy's greeting.

"Yes, this is she."

"Mrs. Renard, is everything all right with Megan?"

"Who is this?"

"I'm sorry, this is Nancy, the choir director up at Centennial Elementary."

"Oh hello, Nancy. Yes, everything's fine. As far as I know, that is. What's up?"

"Well, I thought your daughter was interested in singing?"

"She is. Is there something wrong?"

"Well, Mrs. Renard, we are into the third week now,

and she hasn't been showing up for class. If she doesn't want to be here, I will have to fill her spot. We're trying to get ready for the upcoming fall concert, and I need everyone's involvement to nail it."

Nate walked into the kitchen and poured himself a glass of lemonade. He pretended not to be listening, but you can bet your sweet ass he was. Nate was a good guy, but he was not immune to insecurity. He selectively listened to everything.

"I understand. I had no clue. I wonder where she's been going then?" questioned Brandy.

Nate's ears perked up a little.

"I'm not sure, but she hasn't been here," Nancy said. "During the second week, she came in but snuck out ten minutes into the class each day. I saw her under the bleachers one day, drawing or writing something in a tablet. As I approached her, I was interrupted by one of my students. When I turned back around, Megan was gone. The first week went great. She sang her little heart out. It was her favorite song, or so she said. She sang it beautifully. I gave her a lead in the program because of it. Now we're into the third week and, well, there's no sign of her."

"I'm so sorry, Nancy. I—I will get to the bottom of this and call you back."

"Very well. I hope everything is all right. I hate to lose that voice of hers, but I'm running out of time. I may have to replace her soon."

The other end of the line went dead before any goodbyes were exchanged. Brandy still held the phone to her ear in bewilderment for a second or two before hanging the phone on the receiver. She wondered what in hell was going on.

"Everything all right, dear?" Nathan meekly asked, sipping his lemonade. He was concerned with the half of the conversation he'd heard, as well as the strange look that fell upon Brandy's face at the end of the conversation.

"Oh hi, Nate, I didn't..."

"Yeah, I know," he interrupted. "The phone call? Is everything cool?"

"No, no it's not. Seems our little girl has been cutting class."

"Oh?"

"Yes, choir."

"Choir? Then where has she been going? She hasn't been here."

"That's what concerns me. Let's go get her and find out." Brandy looked down at her watch. "We're late. Let's get going."

Nate and Brandy grabbed their jackets and rushed to the car. They were going to be about ten minutes late for picking Megan up at their usual rendezvous.

When they arrived they found Megan sitting cross-legged on the sidewalk, drawing in her sketchpad. She wasn't at all concerned where her parents were, but they sure were about her.

Megan climbed into the backseat and buckled up.

"Hi, Megan, sorry we're late, honey," apologized Brandy.

"That's all right." She continued to stare down at her drawing and drew some more.

Brandy and Nate stole a glance at one another in wonder, unsure how to handle this. No words were exchanged as Nate drove on in silence, but as soon as they arrived at their front door, that all changed.

Nate spoke up first. "So, Megan, how was choir?"

She didn't answer.

"Megan, your father asked you a question," Brandy said firmly.

Megan knew better than to lie to her father, so she chose the silent treatment once more.

"Megan!" Brandy raised her voice to gain Megan's attention.

"It was fine," she answered sharply.

"Oh? What did you sing today?" her mother inquired.

"'Like a Tattoo.'"

"Again?"

"Yes, it's my favorite song."

"But didn't you learn that song the first day you were

there?"

"Yes, I sing it everyday." Megan tried hard to avoid an all-out lie.

"Megan, is there something you would like to tell us?"

"No, Mom. Why?"

"Well, because your choir director called today, which, by the way, was why we were late picking you up."

Megan's eyes widened. "Oh?"

"She said you've been cutting class."

Megan got quiet again.

"Where have you been, Megan?" Nate said, an octave lower. "We know you haven't been there, and you haven't been here either."

She still wasn't talking. Brandy turned to face her. She took hold of both of Megan's arms. "Go to your room, and don't come out until you feel like talking."

"But..."

"No buts. Tell us where you've been or go to your room," Brandy cut her off.

Not another word was said. Megan simply turned and walked to her room, slamming the door behind her. Nate and Brandy just stood there, mouths agape, looking at each other.

"What do you think that was all about?" Nate asked.

Brandy shrugged. "I'll talk to her later. Let's let her think for a while."

Brandy paced back and forth for hours. Every now and then, she would place an ear up against Megan's bedroom door. More than a few times, she heard the rustling of papers, but even that had stopped after a while. She figured Megan must have fallen asleep.

It was nearly dinnertime, and Brandy was in the kitchen struggling to find something to fix. Her head was wrapped around the problems at hand, and deep inside a cupboard, when she heard Megan's bedroom door creak open. She rubbernecked around the cupboard door just in time to see Megan head down the hallway. She heard the bathroom door shut and lock. Brandy patiently waited just outside the bathroom door, arms folded, back up against the wall.

The latch on the door tumbled and the door slowly opened. Megan's head poked out to see if the coast was clear. It was clear to the right, but when she looked left, her eyes got as big as silver dollars. Startled, she gasped for air when her eyes met her mom's.

"Are you ready to talk?" Brandy asked while her toe was tapping the hardwood floor.

"You scared me," Megan whispered, catching her breath.

Brandy tapped some more. "Sorry, mom, I didn't know how to tell you, but I hate choir."

"Okay, why didn't you just say something instead of not going?"

"I didn't mind going. It's just the songs they chose to sing aren't my kind of songs. That's all."

"But you love 'Tattoo' by Jordin Sparks."

"Yeah, but that's the only one. The rest of the songs they sang were pretty lame."

"Lame?" Brandy chuckled at her word choice. "Then what did you do? Where did you go?"

"Different places, not far. I would just find a quiet place to sit and sketch and write. Sometimes I'd go under the bleachers, other times in the school library."

"I see. Well, thanks for telling me, Megan. You know you can talk to me about anything, don't you? Anything at all."

"I know, Mom. I just didn't want to disappoint you."

The next day Brandy called and broke the news to the choir director.

Nancy's phone rang. "Hello."

"Hello, Nancy?"

"Yes."

"This is Mrs. Renard. I'm calling about my daughter, Megan. I talked to you yesterday."

"Yes, Mrs. Renard, did you straighten things out with your daughter?"

"Yes, I did, Nancy."

"Great! So there won't be any more issues?"

"No, Nancy, there won't be. I'm sorry to say that Megan will no longer be attending your class."

"Oh good—wait, *what*? Why is that?"

"No offense, Nancy, but she just didn't care for it, that's all. I just wanted to let you know so you have time to replace her."

A long silence filled the handset before Brandy's earpiece exploded with anger. "Un-frickin'-believable! I can't believe she would do this to me. I have less than three weeks until the concert. How can I find someone so quickly? This has put me in a terrible situation, Mrs. Renard. I hope you'll discipline accordingly!"

Brandy placed the phone back to her ear. "Discipline? I'm not going to discipline her for not wanting to be involved in choir. That's totally up to her."

"Really? She's really put me out, Mrs. Renard. She needs to be punished!"

"I'm sorry, Nancy, but how dare you tell me how to raise my child! I can see why she didn't enjoy your class. Goodbye!" Brandy hung the phone up without waiting for a reply. "The nerve of people," she growled. "I hope you like book club, Megan," she said to herself.

Book club couldn't have been a more perfect fit for Megan. She loved the fact that she didn't have to stay there to read, and that she could read any book she wanted. They met once a week to share what they had read and, at times, would swap books with one another, which made for an unlimited supply of material. It was perfect for her, and it never pulled her away from her own backyard.

Megan would come home and spend hours on end leaning up against the trunk of the tree in the backyard, reading aloud to whoever cared to listen. Charlie, the garden gnome, for example, probably had more listening hours under his belt than any other gnome in the world.

When it rained, Megan would sit at the kitchen table and read or write, and even draw pictures of what she saw out in the backyard. She was so much like her brother that way.

•••

CHAPTER 7

The sound of air brakes could barely be heard over the low roar coming from the kids riding in the back of the bus.

"I'm not going to say it again, kids," the driver barked over the PA speaker. "You in the back of the bus, stay in your seats and *shut up*, or I'll turn the bus around and head back to the garage!"

Silence quickly filled the air as the kids came to attention.

"What an ass! He doesn't even know how to drive," one of the boys in the back said quietly. Kids within earshot chuckled. The driver peered back through the rearview mirror, as if he'd heard the remark and knew who'd said it.

A small voice, oblivious to her surroundings, continued a conversation with herself.

"Shhhhh, shhhhhhh everyone, I'm trying to hear," another boy at the back of the bus whispered over the nearby murmurs.

"Hear what?" asked yet another.

"Megan, my neighbor. Up about three rows. I swear she said something about an ash tree in her backyard."

"Yeah, I heard that. She talks about it all the time," another jock said. They were all wearing their football jerseys from a school assembly held earlier in the day. They were seniors, and the bus had just picked up the elementary school kids.

"Well, my dad would be pissed if he found out. We had to chop our ash trees down. We had three of them. It cost him big bucks, man. We almost couldn't come up with this year's football fees because of it."

"Are you going to tell him?"

"Hell yeah, I'm going to tell him! Anything I can get on them for what they did to my brother will be brownie points for me. My dad can't stand the prissy-asses next door. Their son killed himself years ago because people teased him for being a retard, and they blamed my older brother and now he's serving time."

"He wasn't retarded," another boy said. "He had something wrong with his lip or something. I remember him. My sister always talked about him."

"Yeah, whatever. He was a retard."

The boys laughed as the bus pulled over to the side of the road to let some kids off. "Hey, isn't that your stop?" the other boy asked.

"Yeah, but I'm going over to Jay's house to hang. You should come. His parents are going to be gone, and they have beer in the fridge."

"Oh man, I can't. Maybe another time."

"Beer's in the fridge, dude. Really?"

"Well, all right, I'll tell my dad tomorrow. I just can't wait to see the look on his face when I do. It's going to be epic. The retard's folks are going to pay."

"Hey now, that was kind of uncalled for, don't you think?"

"What? He's gone, what's he going to do, come back and haunt me?"

"Dude, uncool. His sister is sitting right up there. Now keep it down, ass."

"Ass? Really, you called me an ass? I'll say whatever the hell I want to say, punk!"

That's where it began. Push quickly came to shove, and, shortly after, fists started to fly. Bodies tumbled over the backs of the padded bus seats and bounced back for more. The two fought tirelessly, and things got rougher and more serious by the second. The bus driver's wide eyes could be seen a mile away in the review mirror as he helplessly watched on, all the while trying to keep the bus under control on the uneven grade. He pulled the bus over to the side of the road again. The bus bounced and shook across the gravel and finally came to a jerky stop.

The sudden stop threw some of the kids to their knees, while throwing others hard against the seats in front of them, ultimately dumping a few to the floor. It also seemed to fuel the fire a little more as the noise grew louder and louder. More and more kids cheered the fight on, pushing the two into one another like a human cage. Some kids made their way to the front of the bus to get out of harm's way, while others stayed, ducking low in their seats as fists, arms, and legs flew above their heads.

"Guys, guys! Man, you don't want to do this," one of their teammates said. "We have a game Friday night, and we need you both! You have to stop, they'll bench ya, or worse, expel you from school and off the team."

For a second or two, the two fighters stopped to listen to what their teammate was saying; it made a lot of sense, at least temporarily. But as soon as another opening presented itself, it was too late. The first-string star quarterback pulled back and sucker-punched the first-string receiver in the face with all of his might. The hit threw the boy over the seat he was leaning against, and thrust his head hard against the window, knocking it, and him, out. The window folded and flopped to the ground outside the bus as it was designed to do. The star receiver didn't fare well at all. After impact, his limp body sank into the seat and slithered onto the floor like a rag doll.

The fight was over. What seemed like minutes had

taken place in mere seconds, and silence once again filled the air of the bus. The heavy-set driver struggled to find the seatbelt under his big gut. In all his nervousness, his fat thumb passed over the release button multiple times, before pressing it to release. He pushed the button and wiggled the latch free at the same time the struck boy's limp body fell to the floor. A big sucking sound of air could be heard as all the kids gasped in sync, not believing what they had just witnessed.

Quickly, the kids turned in their seats and faced the front of the bus as they saw the driver attempt to push his way down the aisle. He tried his best to get there before someone got killed, but his thunderous hips slowed his progress as they smacked hard against each seat at the edge of the aisle. He finally maneuvered his way to the back. He stopped to wipe his brow with a hanky as sweat poured from his face and onto the seats below.

When he got to the scene, with little effort the driver physically tossed the star quarterback back into his seat, as he was the only one who remained standing, staring down at his handiwork as if he were in a trance. The driver then turned to see the bloody mess.

Blood streaked down the side of the wall under the missing window and trailed down to a motionless body crumpled on the bus floor. Blood was spattered on the seats, coats, and book bags. Kids started to cry when they finally realized that the boy could be seriously hurt.

The driver looked down at the kid on the floor, who appeared to be unconscious. He bent down and checked for a pulse, then stuck his eyeglasses in front of the boy's mouth and nose. The glasses fogged a little, bringing a little relief to the driver's face.

The driver, now wide-eyed and frantic, wasn't trained for such a situation, but he knew enough not to move the body. Out of breath himself, he struggled to pull himself back to his feet.

"Everyone stay in your seats and keep quiet!" he barked, using the remainder of his breath and energy. He made his way up to the driver's seat, running on pure adrenaline. When he arrived, he was panting like a dog and gasping for all the air his lungs could hold. He flipped a couple of switches on the radio with one hand and grabbed the mic with the other.

"This is bus #2623 in need of emergency assistance," he said, gasping for air.

"Bus #2623 go ahead, all others keep channel clear," the dispatcher replied.

"Fight on the bus," he said, taking another breath. "Boy down, unconscious under seats. Location: Fifth Street near Mackin. Send help."

"Hang tight, Mac, ambulance en route. Is the situation under control?"

"Affirmative. I already hear the sirens. Out," Mac answered back.

"Bus 2623?"

"2623 go ahead," Mac answered.

"Is there blood at the scene?"

"Roger that, and lots of it."

"Please evacuate the bus to a safe location and await a new bus arrival. Dispatching now."

"Roger that. EMT just arrived. Out."

The driver met the paramedics just outside the bus door and directed them to the downed victim.

One of the medics noticed the sweat pouring down the driver's face. "Are you all right, sir? Why don't you sit down over there in the grass?" By now a crowd started gathering, gawking from nearby yards.

"I'm fine. I need to evacuate the bus."

"No, you need to sit down before you fall down." The paramedic noticed a shake in the driver's legs and guided him to the grass. He helped the driver down to the ground. A few more seconds and the driver wouldn't have needed any help. The medic began checking his vitals.

"Sir, I'm fine. Tend to the boy on the bus. He's in bad shape."

"Mark is taking care of him," the medic said, gesturing toward his partner already on the bus.

Mark appeared at the doorway shortly after that. "Whatcha got?" he asked.

"Just checking him over. He didn't look so hot. You got

the kid?"

Mark shook his head. "We need these kids off the bus."

"Shit!" said the other medic.

"Shit? What? Oh my gosh, no," said the driver. He tried to get up but was tied up with the blood pressure band. He started ripping it off.

"No, no, no. That cuff stays and so do you, or you're going to join him. Do you understand me? You're under a lot of stress, and that's not real good for you right now. You need to relax and just take it easy, and let us do our jobs. "

Just then, the replacement bus drove up and parked behind the first. The driver of that bus jogged up to see if he could help.

Mark immediately pulled him aside and filled him in. "We have a boy down in the second to the last seat on the right. He's DOA. There's blood everywhere. We need to get the kids off the bus and onto yours ASAP, with minimal commotion and without them knowing. Can you do that?"

The driver nodded and immediately boarded the bus. Mark squeezed past him and pretended to be helping the downed victim.

"Is he all right? Is he going to be all right?" kids asked as they walked by.

It was loud and getting unruly. The new driver pulled a whistle from a chain around his neck and blew. The ear-piercing trill cut the air like a foghorn. Kids covered their ears; some cried out, unsure what was happening.

"Can I have your attention?" the new driver yelled. "Please, give them room, and let the medics do their job. We are going to get off this bus right now, and single-file it over to the bus parked directly behind us. There will be no pushing, no shoving, and no talking!" He paused, "Now, look down at your belongings. If you see blood on it, leave it. If not, grab it and let's go! *Now!*"

The kids grabbed what was theirs and started marching down the aisle. A little girl screamed loudly when she noticed her purse was spattered with blood. She threw it back down in her seat. Heads turned in her direction. Her body shook.

The kids gasped when they stepped off the bus and saw their driver, Mac, on the ground with another medic.

"Are you all right?" asked a little girl walking alongside the bus.

"No talking!" barked the new driver. The little girl cringed. Mac nodded back to say he was okay.

The kids got settled on the new bus while the new driver jogged back to the old. "You all right?" he asked Mac as he passed by.

Now wearing an oxygen mask, Mac nodded as the plastic mask he was wearing fogged up. The new driver then climbed back aboard the evacuated bus and grabbed the clipboard hanging behind the driver's seat. It was the manifest and list of stops.

He then ran back to his own bus and got on the PA.

"Can I have your attention, please?" The driver paused, waiting for the kids to simmer down. "I don't know what happened back there on your bus, but I can guarantee you that it will not happen here on mine. The medics are doing everything they can for your friend and for Mac. Now, I could use some assistance. I do not know your stops. Will the last stop come up to the front seat of the bus and help me so I can get you kids home safely? Your parents have all been texted, notifying them that you are going to be a little late."

Two boys and a girl walked up the aisle and sat in the front row. "Thanks, kids. Who knows the stops?" Two of the three raised their hands. "Great!" The driver merged onto the road.

It wasn't long before two marked and one unmarked police cars pulled up behind the parked bus. Two more followed moments later, along with the coroner.

"What the hell?" asked the driver, while sitting on the ground, pulling his oxygen mask off.

"Leave that on, sir, it's procedure."

"I'm all right. I don't need..."

"Please, sir, let us do our job."

The driver refused and rocked himself to his feet. Uniformed officers met him at the door of the bus.

"Sir, you can't go on," an officer said.

"I beg your pardon. This is my bus, and I will go on it if I want to."

"It may be your bus, but it's also a crime scene." The officer pulled a roll of yellow police tape from a pouch and started to tape off the scene.

"Crime scene? It was just two kids getting into a fight. Happens every day."

"That may be true, sir, but not every day one of them dies." Shocked, the driver backed away, clutching his fist against his chest. "Medic!" the officer yelled to the paramedic, pointing to the bus driver.

Mac collapsed to the ground just as the medic got there. His vitals were good, and it appeared the driver just passed out. Two officers helped the medics get the driver up onto a gurney and into the ambulance. Another was called to the scene for the boy's body.

An officer followed the ambulance to the hospital, hoping to get a statement once the driver was stable and well enough to talk. Once checked in and checked over, the big man eagerly cooperated and told the cop everything he knew. A few hours later, he was released to go home.

•••

CHAPTER 8

Megan stepped off the school bus and straight into Brandy's arms. Brandy mouthed the words, "thank you" to the driver as he closed the door and pulled away. "Are you all right?" she asked Megan, concerned over the text she'd received from the school about the incident on the bus. They went inside to talk. Neither the text nor Megan went into much detail. Brandy just knew that a fight had broken out between two of the kids, and one was taken to the hospital. Megan seemed fine, though, and went right to her room to play.

After reading Brandy's text, Nate went to mow the lawn. It was something he always did to deal with stress. There was something about power tools and cutting things that always seemed to calm his nerves.

Brandy heard loud bang coming from the backyard while Nathan was out mowing. It was a so loud that it could be heard for blocks. It was even loud behind closed doors, as Brandy, sitting on the couch in the living room, thought it was a gunshot and jumped to her feet. The pitter-patter of racing little feet skidded to a stop in Brandy's arms, as she braced herself for impact in a catcher's stance.

Frightened by the sound, Megan cried out. "What was that, Mom?!"

"It's all right, it was probably nothing," Brandy said, making her way to the kitchen and dragging Megan along by her arm. She pulled the sliding door open and walked outside onto the deck. Brandy motioned to Nate to come over.

"Yeah?" Nate yelled over the roar of the lawn mower.

"What was that loud noise?" Brandy yelled.

Nate motioned to his ear, shaking his head. He couldn't hear her. He finished one more pass with the lawn mower, hitting that same shallow root once again. "BANG!"

"Dang it!" Nate yelled. The engine stalled out this time. Instead of restarting it, he assessed the damage.

Two large chunks of wood were shaved off the shallow main root of the tree. They lay on the ground just yards away from the root that snaked across the lawn. Nate flipped the lawn mower over to check out the blades. "Good, still okay," he muttered under his breath. "As for the tree, on the other hand, oh boy."

Nate looked up at Brandy and Megan standing on the deck, grave concern written all over Megan's face. "What did you say?" he asked.

"That bang? It just scared Megan, that's all."

"Oh, it's nothing. I keep hitting a root of the tree. It looks like I got it pretty good this time. I'll check at the nursery for something to put on it later."

Megan gasped and covered her mouth. Tears quickly filled her eyes.

"Oh, all right. Dinner will be ready soon." Brandy looked down at Megan and noticed her tears.

"I'm almost done," Nate said. "I just want to trim a few of these low branches, and then I'll be in."

"Oh, all right."

Brandy turned to Megan. "What's wrong, honey?" she asked, while wiping some tears away with her thumbs.

Megan shook her head, pointing to where Nate hit the root. Two bright white patches of wood glared up from the ground where they lay.

"Oh, the tree? It will be all right, Megan. It's just a root."

Megan turned to look at the base of the tree. "Daddy hurt him," she said.

"No, Megan. The tree will be fine, I promise."

Nate came out of the garage with some pruners and started cutting some low-hanging branches. "Man, this tree can be messy," he said as he dropped the first branch to the ground.

"He's hurting him, he's hurting him! Make him stop. Please, Mom, make Daddy stop," Megan cried out as her father moved to the next branch, clipping it off just above his head.

Nate heard Megan's cries and stopped just as the branch hit the ground. "What's wrong with her?"

"She thinks you're hurting the tree, I guess."

"Well, that's silly. I'm just trimming it, Meg." Nate reached up and cut another branch down, then lined up for yet another.

Megan screamed bloody murder. "Daddy's hurting Ash!" She then ran into the house, down the hall, and into her room. She buried herself under the covers of her bed.

Brandy's eyes couldn't have gotten bigger. Her mouth dropped open and was quickly covered with her hand. She looked at Nate and then bolted after her daughter.

When she entered Megan's room, she noticed a large lump in the middle of the bed. "Megan? What did you say, dear?"

"Daddy is hurting the tree." She threw back the covers and pointed out the window. "Look!" They both could see Nathan removing more branches from the tree, one after another.

"Honey, he's just trimming it. It's all right."

"No, it's hurting him, it's hurting him," Megan repeated. Brandy opened the window and ordered Nate to stop and come in. "We have a problem!"

Nate dropped the trimmer and ran inside. "What's up?"

"It's Megan, she thinks you're hurting the tree."

"I'm just..."

"I know, but she ran to her room screaming, 'you're hurting him, you're hurting him.'"

"Him?" Nate shrugged.

"Yes, him, and that's not all. She said his name again."

"Really? That's impossible. How?"

"You tell me," said Brandy.

"I've never said one word."

"Well, neither have I."

"Megan, honey, I'm just trimming the tree. It doesn't hurt it. It's like when you get a hair cut. It doesn't hurt when someone cuts your hair, does it?"

Megan just stared off into the distance with watery eyes.

"Who do you think I'm hurting?" Nate continued.

Megan clammed up. She wasn't talking. Then out of nowhere, she ran out to the great room and pointed to the framed picture high up on the bookshelf.

Nathan and Brandy just stood looking at each other, puzzled. Brandy's heart was in her throat. "I think it's time," she said.

Nate nodded.

Brandy reached up and brought down the photo and showed it to Megan. "Do you know who this is?"

Megan nodded her head, confirming she did. Her

confidence confused her parents even more.

"Who is it, Megan?" Brandy asked.

Megan still wasn't talking.

"Who is in the picture, honey?" reiterated Nate, squatting down to her level.

"That's my brother, Ash," Megan said, this time without hesitation.

Brandy felt dizzy, lightheaded even. She had to sit down before she fell down.

"Who told you his name?" asked Nate.

"He did," she answered.

"He?"

Megan pointed to the tree in the backyard.

Now it was Nate's turn to take a seat. He sat and shook his head in disbelief.

"Megan, please honey, you have to tell us how you knew," Brandy said. "Did you hear Mommy and Daddy talking about him?"

"No, Mom."

"Friends?" Brandy asked, realizing she had none. Megan shook her head no.

"How about the neighbor?" Megan got a strange look on her face when Brandy mentioned the neighbor. Then she started to cry.

"No, no don't, it's all right, honey. You're not in any

trouble. We just want to know how, that's all," Nate said in a consoling manner.

"It's how the fight got started on the bus," she said.

"What?" Nate and Brandy said simultaneously.

"Our neighbor was saying bad things about Ashton, and another boy stood up for him. I heard them talking. They were talking about Ash. One said that he was retarded and the other didn't like it."

"Honey, I'm so sorry," consoled Brandy. She gave Meg a long hug. "But that was just yesterday."

"I've known for a long time, Mom."

"How, honey?"

"Ash told me. We talk pretty much every day."

"Honey," Brandy paused not knowing how to ask. "Is Ash your imaginary friend? Is that who you talk to all the time in the backyard?"

"Yes, Mom, but he's not imaginary. Ash is for real."

Again Nate and Brandy found themselves staring at each other, dumbfounded.

"Yes, of course he's for real," Brandy agreed.

"He asked me to give you two something." Brandy and Nate shrugged at each other, wide-eyed.

"I'll be right back." Megan ran to her room and brought back a sketchpad. She ripped out a sheet and gave it to them. "This is from Ash."

It was the note that Ash didn't have a chance to finish

himself. Brandy swallowed hard and began to read it out loud.

Dear Mom & Dad,

Please forgive me, and please believe it was nothing that you've done. You weren't perfect parents, but you were perfect for me. I'm sorry if you hurt, but my pain, for once, is gone, and I am free. Hopefully, in time, you will understand if you don't already.

Your son, Ashton

P.S. Megan is a cool sister.

"What is this? Is someone playing a trick on us? Who wrote this anyway?" Nate questioned doubtfully.

"Megan, honey, who wrote the note? Did you write this? How did you know about Ash?" She paused. "And what exactly do you know about him?"

Megan said nothing, but her eyes told a different story. They were filled with fear and bewilderment. She didn't understand why her own parents didn't believe her. She searched high and low for a different answer, one that she thought would be more acceptable, but she just couldn't come up with one, so she told what she knew to be true.

"He's my brother, and he told me," she answered.

"This isn't funny," said Nate, irritated to no end. "How could she possibly know any of this, especially the note and what he looked like? She recognized his picture, for Pete's sake. You must have told her something."

"Me? I told her nothing!" Brandy defended. "This was our little secret."

"Then explain this, will ya? Would you please explain what the hell is happening here? Because what I'm hearing goes against everything that I believe in." Nate paced back and forth across the room.

"Me too, but what if she's telling the truth? What if she can talk to Ash?"

"No, no, I'm not hearing this. Seriously, Brandy? You actually believe any of this. Somebody's playing a sick joke on us, and it's not a bit funny."

Megan's gaze ping-ponged back and forth between her mom and dad as they argued, which confused her more than ever. She began to cry. The tears rolled down her cheeks and dropped to the floor, stopping her parents' argument in its tracks.

"Megan, please, honey, tell us how you knew that was Ash in the picture. Please, we won't be mad. Just tell us the truth," Brandy pleaded.

Megan caught her breath. "Because. It looks just like the boy in the tree," she answered.

Silence fell as Nate and Brandy froze and stared wide-eyed again at each other.

"That tree? Out there?" Nathan, breaking his stare

asked her while pointing out the slider to the backyard.

Megan nodded.

"Will you show us?" asked Brandy.

Megan led the way out the back door and down the ramp of the deck. She stopped right in front of the tree and pointed to a spot on the north side. Nate and Brandy just stared at the location a moment and shrugged at each other.

"Where?" Brandy asked. She obviously wasn't seeing anything. Megan pointed to the face in the photo in her mother's hand. She pointed specifically toward the lip area, while pointing to the location on the tree again.

"You have to believe," Megan whispered.

Just then, and only for a split second, Brandy thought she saw it, as did Nate. For that brief moment they did see it, and at that point in time, they saw nothing else. Sure enough, there was indeed a face in the bark of the tree, and it bore quite a likeness to their deceased little boy in the picture.

Nate began to rub his eyes in disbelief, as the image slowly faded away. A moment later it disappeared for Brandy as well; then it was gone.

They both had seen it, but they didn't believe their own eyes, and the mind will never see what the mind refuses to believe.

Nate shook his head, then stared back at the tree again. He placed his hand on the bark where he thought he had seen his son's face. Then he turned to Megan. "You say he talked to you?"

She nodded.

Brandy began to tear up, wanting so badly to believe, but her adult mind got in the way. *Ash?* she questioned herself.

"Can you make him talk?" Nate questioned.

"It doesn't work that way, silly. He's not a parrot," Megan said. "When he has something to say, he simply puts words in my head."

"Well, what is he saying, now?"

"Nothing, Dad. He's not saying a word. You don't believe."

"I'm trying to, honey. I really am."

The family spent the evening on the deck that night. They cooked dinner on the grill, and they waited for Ash to say something to Megan, but the words never came.

Doubting, Nate struck again. "Fairy tales," he grumbled to himself.

The next morning it rained, not hard, but a steady drizzle. Like usual, Nathan was the first out of bed, but not for the normal reasons. He was awakened multiple times during the night by the same dream. He dreamt he talked to Ash, but each time he awoke, he could never remember what was said.

Nathan didn't bother getting dressed, so there he was,

standing under the tree with an umbrella, in his bathrobe. He knew what he had seen the day before, and he was bound and determined to see it again. He stared long and hard at the tree, running his hand over the rough bark.

"What are you doing out there, Nate? It's raining," Brandy said from the open doorway. She wrapped her robe tightly around her waist.

"He's gone. We both saw it, and it's gone."

Brandy didn't know what to say. Hearing a noise, she turned around. Megan was standing behind her.

"What's going on, Mom?" she asked while rubbing the sleep from her eyes.

"It's your dad. I think he's trying to contact Ashton."

Megan smiled. The rain had stopped, and they stepped outside together and stood by Nate.

"Are you all right, dear?" Brandy asked, rubbing his back.

"I talked to him last night."

"You talked to Ashton?"

"Yeah, a few times."

"What? How?"

"They were dreams. I can't explain it. I don't even remember what was said. I was just hoping he would be here this morning."

"He doesn't come out in the rain, Daddy."

"No? Why not?"

"Not sure, he just never has. Maybe he doesn't like getting wet."

"It is just trickery. That's all it is. Trickery." Nate hung his head and walked away.

Megan began to cry.

"Nate... Nathan!" Brandy's plea was cut short by the sliding door slamming hard against the doorframe behind him.

Brandy chased after Nate, leaving Megan holding the umbrella. The sliding glass door slammed behind Brandy as well.

"Don't walk away from me when I'm talking to you," she told her husband. "Now, do you want to tell me what the hell that was all about?"

"What? What do you want from me, Brandy? Do you want me to believe in ghosts and fairy tales? Believe in something I don't understand? She's lost it!"

"She's just a little girl," Brandy said, gritting her teeth. "Now, I don't know what's going on either. I don't know what's real, but whether it's real or not, or just in her imagination, it's real to her. We both saw the image of the face yesterday. You saw it. Don't deny it."

"Maybe we only saw what we wanted to see, Brandy, and after we got some sleep and our minds cleared, reality took over again."

"That might be true, Nate, but for now, until we know

what is happening, we have to support our daughter. Right now it's all we have that might explain what she knows."

The only sound breaking the silence between them was Brandy's panting breath. Nate thought for a minute. "You're right. I'm sorry. I shouldn't have left. What do we do now?"

"I don't know. We need to seek help. But where?"

Nate looked out at Megan. "She's talking to him again. Look."

They both stood behind the glass, looking out of the fishbowl into what they now thought of as Megan's fantasy world.

Brandy motioned for Nate to open the door. "We should go out."

Nathan opened the door and stepped out. Brandy followed close behind.

The sun was shining brightly on the tree. It wasn't long before the tree was completely dry, allowing the image to once again show its face.

"Nate, look. It's back," said Brandy.

Nathan couldn't believe his eyes, but it was there as clear as day. They made their way to the tree. Nate wrapped his arm around Megan and said hello to Ash.

"He said hello back, Dad," Megan replied for Ashton.

Nate looked down at Megan, then up at Brandy. Eyes wide, he nodded.

"Hi, Ash. How are you?" asked Brandy, trying to play

along, trying hard to believe.

"He said hello, Mom, and that he's fine and misses you."

Goosebumps appeared on Brandy's arms. She tried to stifle the chill that ran up her spine. Her eyes began to tear up.

"Tell us, Ash. What's it like?" asked Nathan.

"It's peaceful, Dad. No one is calling me names and pushing me down. I no longer have to fight to live. I'm all right, Dad," Ash said through Megan's mind. Megan repeated it back aloud.

"Why does he have to talk through you? Why not to us?"

"You have to fully believe, Dad. Right now you're just trying," she answered.

Brandy tried hard to think of a question that Megan wouldn't know. "Ash, I'm sorry, but your dog passed away about a year after you did."

"He said he knew about the gate, Mom. He tried to shut it, but it was just out of reach of his branches. He knew something happened when he stopped seeing her out in the backyard doing his business. Then he watched Dad bury Sparky behind the garage," said Megan. Then she asked, "We had a dog? What kind? Can we have another dog? Please, please, can we?"

Chills returned again to Brandy's body. She was feeling

faint and started to sit down before she fell down. Nate was feeling a bit queasy himself and sat down next to her. He held her tight.

"Well? Can we?" Megan asked again.

Brandy and Nate both forgot the question.

"Can we what, dear," her dad asked.

"A dog. Can we get a dog?" Meg asked again.

"We'll think about it, hon," he answered.

"Nathan, that was over eight years ago. There's no possible..."

"I know, dear. I know," interrupted Nate.

"One more thing, Nate."

"What's that, dear," he questioned.

"The fight on the bus. It's all over Facebook that the boy died. He died because he defended our daughter and Ash."

"Yeah, I caught that too," Nate replied with a tear in his eye. "Find out more information, will you? We need to talk to that family."

•••

CHAPTER 9

After Megan was born, the nightmares had pretty much stopped for Brandy. She used to dream about Ashton all the time. Some bad dreams, some good, but most were just plain horrific and weren't considered dreams at all. They had their own classification, their own term. they were called night terrors.

The night terrors would wake Brandy up, breathless and in cold sweats. She would roll over, toss and turn all night, and sometimes scream so loud that she could wake the neighbors. Nate would have to shake her awake in fear she would hurt something, mainly herself, during her most violent fits. The first year after Ash's death was the worst. She had to take sleeping pills in order to get any rest at all. Hell, in order for Nate to get any at all.

Many nights, Brandy would send Nate off to bed without her, in fear of having another attack. That's what she called them: "attacks," visions attacking her brain. Nathan hated to leave her alone on the couch, but she never seemed to have them when she slept there.

Now it seemed to be Nate's turn.

"Nate! Nathan, honey, wake up," Brandy called as she prodded him awake. "Nate, you're having a dream."

Nate, covered with sweat, groggily answered, "huh, what, oh," then fell back to sleep, only to be awakened by his wife again and again.

At 5:25 a.m., Nate's alarm went off as he stood in the living room in his boxers, stretching and scratching what was left of the mop on his head. He yawned when he spoke, sounding a bit like a beached whale. "Whyyyy arrrrrrre youuuuu out herrrrrrre? You're not having those dreams again, are you?

Brandy, facing the back of the couch, rolled over. "Not me. You tossed, turned, and kicked like a mule last night. I can't wait to count my bruises."

"That was quite a storm last night, huh? I better have a look around before I go in to work."

"Nate, it didn't storm last night."

"It did so. You didn't hear it? The wind was whipping, lightning, thunder, the works." Nate pulled the shades back from the window and looked outside. "Hmm, dry as a bone out there. Wait a minute." A scene from the dream he'd had flashed before his eyes. He ran to the kitchen and looked out that window to the tree in the backyard. "Wow, it must have been a dream." Nate seemed shaken.

"What was it, dear?"

"In the dream the tree took a direct lightning hit and fell over onto the house. It crashed through the ceiling and did thousands of dollars worth of damage. When I looked out the window, I saw this shadow of a boy standing in the middle of the hollowed stump left behind. It was Ashton, surrounded by charred bark. Smoke rose all around him. He just stared at me in the window, trying to get me to help him, but I couldn't move. I just stared back, until..."

"Until what? Until what, Nate?"

"I don't know, I must have woke up. That's all I remember." Nate sat at the edge of the couch with his elbows on his knees. Brandy hugged him from behind and rubbed his back.

"What do you think it means?" asked Nate.

"I'm not much into interpreting dreams, but my guess would be that you're starting to believe and your imagination is taking over."

A few minutes passed, and Nate rubbed more sleep from his eyes. "I'm going to be late. I have to get ready." He stood and walked into the other room.

Brandy just watched as he walked away. She knew that the dream really bothered him, but she didn't know what to say.

•••

CHAPTER 10

Going against doctor's orders, Mac felt good enough to show up for work the next morning. When he got there, to his surprise, a closed-door meeting was taking place in his honor. Mac had a bad feeling about it when he let himself in.

"Mac!" the bus superintendent exclaimed, surprised to see him. "C-c-come in," she nervously stuttered, confirming Mac's suspicions.

"What's this all about?" Mac asked.

"Please, sit."

"I can't. I have to get on my run."

"Don't worry about your run today, Mac. We've got you covered. You're not supposed to be here."

"Yeah, I know, but I feel fine. You got me covered?" Mac said, not liking the sound of that at all. Mac had driven for the school system for more than 22 years. His stomach churned as he scanned the faces of the room. The committee included a couple of local cops—he recognized them as the same officers who'd responded to the scene—as well as the school principal, the bus superintendent, and a city official. In this case it was Stan, the mayor himself.

A local news crew pulled in while the meeting was taking place. They waited patiently for the mayor to come out for an interview.

"Can you tell us what happened, Mac?" asked the bus superintendent after taking a sip from her coffee.

"I already gave my statement to the police. What's this about?" Mac responded curiously.

"Would you mind telling it again? To us, this time? Please?"

"Sure, but... Oh, all right. Where do I start?"

"How about when the fight erupted. We assume it was a typical day up until then?"

"There's nothing typical about a busload of kids." That brought smiles across the room. Mac continued. "Well, there was a lot of commotion going on. I pulled off the road as quickly as I could, but it was too late. I did what I could."

"That's it? That's your report? Did you see who started the brawl? I assume there were multiples involved?" asked one of the officers.

"All I could see was what I saw through the rearview mirror, which, wasn't much. I was trying to control the bus safely off to the shoulder. Sorry, I can only speculate, and I know you don't want that."

"That is correct, we don't want speculation. So you're saying you didn't see anything?"

"Oh, I saw plenty."

"Plenty?"

"Yes, through the mirror."

"Are we talking in circles here?" asked an officer.

"Mac, please tell us everything you saw. Details," the super interrupted.

"Well, all right. As I said, I was pulling the bus off to the shoulder of the road when it all went down."

"Why were you pulling the bus over, Mac?" asked the super.

"Because of all the commotion. There was a lot of noise. I was going to yell at the kids to be quiet and maybe threaten to turn the bus around."

"Go on..."

Mac nervously looked around the room again. About a half-dozen pairs of eyes stared back at him, making him feel incredibly uncomfortable. "May I have drink?" he requested.

"Absolutely." The super motioned for one of the officers to grab a bottle of water from the small fridge behind them. Mac gladly accepted the drink and wasted no time opening it. He swallowed nearly half of the bottle with the first swig. He wiped his mouth with the back of his hand.

"I'll be honest with you folks. I would love to tell you I

saw everything that happened and point a finger at who's at fault, but I can't. All I saw was a bunch of kids cheering two football players on as they fought."

"And what did you do once the bus stopped rolling."

"Well, I called it in. No, I called while the bus was still moving. I went back there to control the situation."

"And did you?"

"No, sir. I was too late."

"Too late?"

"Yes, the damage was done."

"Damage? We are talking about a kid here, right?"

"Yes, of course we're talking..." Mac paused. "What is going on here?" he asked. "Am I being accused of something?"

"Mac," the principal butted in. "Standard procedures, Mac. We have to investigate, you know?"

"Do I need a lawyer?" Mac looked around the room. "Are any of you lawyers?"

A man in his mid- to late fifties raised a pen.

"Sir, should I have a lawyer here?" Mac asked.

The lawyer shamefully nodded.

Mac turned and walked out of the room. The principal followed.

"Mac, hey, wait up." Mac briefly hesitated but started walking again. "Mac, please."

"You, of all people. I've driven for you for over 20 years, and you do this?"

"I'm sorry, Mac. We just need answers. We've taken a lot of flak here. Lawsuits are being filed left and right."

"I told you everything I know."

"Everything, Mac?"

"What do you want from me? You want my license?"

"No, Mac, just a name."

"A name? I can't give you a name. I'm sorry, sir. I didn't see who started it."

"I'm not asking you what you saw, Mac. What did you hear?"

"The kids were screaming, sir. It was complete chaos."

"Okay, okay. Well, maybe you'll think of something later."

"I doubt it, sir, but if I do, I will come to you first."

"Very well. Thank you, Mac. Oh, I almost forgot. I have to suspend you without pay until the investigation is over."

"Suspend? Sir? Really?"

"Sorry, Mac. Hopefully it won't be for long. It's just standard procedure."

"I figured as much." Mac shook his head, turned, and walked out of the room.

The principal turned as well and left the building in

another direction. He was hoping to avoid what was to come, but to no avail. Reporters bombarded both men the minute they walked outside.

The principal was accosted first.

"Sir, can I have a few words?" asked the reporter.

"The meeting started like a deposition and ended with the driver on suspension without pay until further notice. That is all," the principal said as he continued making strides toward his car.

Mac refused to comment for anyone and bee-lined straight to his car. Because of his size and determined look, he had no problem negotiating the crowd, like Moses parting the Red Sea.

In the days to come, one by one the kids from the bus were sequestered and interviewed by officials. Some voluntarily came forward, while others wanted no involvement at all. Nevertheless, all fingers pointed in one direction: the star quarterback. And when the kids were asked if the bus driver did all he could to prevent what happened, the answers were shocking.

Three days later, Mac was seen walking past the office to pick up his paycheck. The principal flagged him down. He seemed to be expecting him to show up. "Mac, you got a minute?"

"Time is what I have nowadays, boss."

"Great! Come on in." The bus super was also in the office at the time. They were going over the events that the kids had described earlier. "Please have a seat," the principal said while he walked between a couple dozen chairs, positioned to make a short aisle.

Mac followed close behind, pushing the chairs aside as he passed. He then noticed the bus superintendent seated to the left, and nodded. A familiar uneasy feeling started to churn in Mac's gut as he pushed the last chair out of the way so he could walk through. The principal and the super stared at the chairs, now in a shambled mess. Mac noticed and started to place the chairs back in their original positions.

"Mac, that's all right, just leave them. We're done with them anyway," the principal said.

"Oh, all right. Sorry." Mac took a seat next to the bus super and faced the principal.

"Mac," the principal spoke. "We interviewed a lot of kids in the past couple of days, and I just wanted to let you know that, ah, well, they gave us what we needed. They filled in all the blanks and dotted all the i's for us, and we think we know who started the fight."

"Great, then you don't need me anymore?" Mac started to get out of his seat but struggled. The chair lifted off the floor, stuck to his behind. The arms on the chair pinched him in.

The principal and the super looked on with a nod, confirming what they'd heard.

"Yes, Mac, that's just it, we don't."

Mac had a puzzled look on his face. He tried to speak, but nothing came out.

"Mac, we're going to have to let you go."

"What! Let me go? I don't understand." Finally he pushed himself out of the chair.

"We have received a lot of flak, Mac. In fact, the phones haven't stopped ringing. People are saying you didn't do everything you could that day, and the kids, well, they confirmed it."

"I don't understand. I did..."

"They said you couldn't get down the aisle fast enough, Mac. They said that, because of your size, you had a lot of trouble fitting down the aisle."

"Because of my size? Are you frickin' serious?"

"Mac, we're expecting a lot of lawsuits over this. We didn't do enough to protect the kids."

"Are you firing me because I'm fat?"

"Mac, no, it's because you didn't respond fast enough, and a boy died on your watch."

"I got down that aisle with no problem at all!"

"Mac, the chairs you just tried to walk through were spaced out as if they were an aisle on the bus, and we were very lenient. Look at the chairs now. They are scattered. The kids told us that you struggled to get by each row and actually got stuck a couple of times. Some even said that you struggled to find your seat belt." Mac just sat there and stared at the chairs.

"Now, *I'm* not making this a 'fat' issue; *you* are. I'm making it a safety issue, and we're given no choice but to let you go, for the safety of our kids."

Mac hung his head, kicked a chair out of the way, and started for the door. Before he got there, he turned back around to face his bosses. "Mr. Principal, you weren't there. You say you're expecting a lot of lawsuits over this. You now can expect one more. Good day, sir."

•••

CHAPTER 11

The sign on the door read, "Dr. R.J. Higgins, Phd. Therapist."

Nate hesitated and looked at Brandy before knocking. Brandy nodded, then Nate tapped on the door with his knuckles. They entered.

"Nathan, Brandy, thanks for coming in. What can I do for you?" Dr. Higgins greeted.

"Thanks, Doc. It's our daughter. She's seven, and we don't think she's a typical seven-year-old girl," Brandy said.

"Oh? Autistic?"

"I don't know, maybe, but it's different than that," she answered.

"Please, explain." The doctor motioned for them to take a seat.

"Well," she paused as they sat down and fussed with her skirt, tucking it under her legs as she crossed them. "Sorry,"

103

she apologized for the delay. "She doesn't have any friends, for one thing, and she spends way too much time playing outside."

"I see," the doc responded. "Well, I know a lot of parents who would pay big money for kids like that. I usually get kids who spend too much time in front of the television or play too many video games. But too much time outside, now that's a new one. I fail to see a problem."

"Sorry, I'm not explaining this right." Brandy looked to Nate for guidance. He shrugged, blowing air from his cheeks.

"It's not that she doesn't have any friends. She does, but they are all imaginary," Brandy continued.

"Imaginary?"

"Yeah, imaginary," Brandy offered.

"Kids have imaginary friends. That's completely normal. I still fail to see an issue."

"Listen, I'm paying you good money to make sense of this, and all you're saying is that it's perfectly normal? Come on, Doc, talk to us," Nate said.

"Okay, but I really haven't heard anything too abnormal here, except for the lack of interest in video games. There has to be more."

"She talks to trees," Nate and Brandy finally said in unison.

"And the tree supposedly talks back," added Brandy.

"Talks back?" The doc rubbed his chin. "What does a

tree say?"

"It's not like that. We've never heard it ourselves."

"Then how?" The doctor sighed.

"It—the tree—sends messages to our daughter, and then she relays it to us."

"And, let me guess, you play along, but you don't really believe her?"

"Right! We try. We want to. But how can we?"

"Nate, Brandy," the doc said, taking a seat behind his desk. "Has Megan ever lied to you before?"

"No, absolutely not. We've taught her that it's wrong to lie," answered Brandy. "At least we don't think she has."

"Then what makes you believe that she's lying to you now?"

Nate sighed. "So let me get this straight. She talks to trees, and that's supposed to be all right?"

"Trees? There's more than one?"

Nathan turned toward the door. He was ready to leave, but the session wasn't over. Brandy waited for his response before she answered. "Well, actually, no. It's just one tree that we know of, but she talks to other things as well, like the garden gnome. They've become really good friends, actually. She calls him Charlie."

"A garden gnome and a tree. Are there more trees in your yard?" the doctor questioned.

"Yes, we have more trees," Nate said in frustration. "Why? For Pete's sake, come on, Brandy. I've had enough of this quack."

Brandy struggled. She wasn't leaving without answers, and Nate, well, he was just too busy being Nate. He just wanted to leave because he wasn't hearing what he came there to hear. He was looking for a fix, maybe a pill that Megan could take to stop all this nonsense.

Nate reached for Brandy's hand and turned again for the door. But the doctor's next question stopped him in his tracks.

"Is there something you folks aren't telling me about this particular tree?"

Nate and Brandy both turned and faced the doc with the deer-in-the-headlights look. "Why?" Brandy asked.

"I feel like there is something you're not telling me. What kind of tree is it?"

They both looked at each other and shrugged their shoulders. "It's just a tree," Nate said.

"Well, is it a pine? Birch? Maple?" He paused, waiting for an answer. "Well?"

"We have a birch in the front yard," said Brandy. "That's the kind that are white and peel off like paper, isn't it?"

"That's correct, Brandy, but what about the one Megan talks to?"

"I'm sorry, we don't know. We're not much into trees. Now, our first child, Ashton, could have told you exactly what it is. He knew everything about nature, but he's gone."

"Gone?"

"He died about nine years ago," answered Brandy.

"Oh, I'm so sorry."

"That's all right," Nathan butted in. "Can we move on and get back to the issue at hand, please?"

"Very well, but I'm still waiting."

"For what? What exactly are you waiting for, Doc?" barked Nate.

"What you're not telling me." The doctor stared into a notebook while he jotted down some notes.

Nathan and Brandy were speechless. They didn't know what to say or where to start. The doc finally looked up from his notes. Looking over his round spectacles, he opened his hands wide, prodding an answer. "Was there some kind of accident?" he asked. "Did your son fall from that tree? Is that how he died? There has to be something, and I have a feeling it's about your son."

"Why do you say that?" Nate said defensively. "We didn't come here to talk about our son and your psychic abilities."

"Oh, I'm no mind reader, but you didn't come here to talk about a tree either. I feel they have something in common," said the doc.

Nate and Brandy never talked about it and hadn't told anyone. It was to be their own little secret, and they struggled to keep it that way, even from the therapist.

"Oh, all right. No one knows this, so your doctor-patient confidentiality better be damn good!" threatened Brandy.

The doc pushed his glasses up the bridge of his nose, nodded his head, and listened, bright-eyed.

"I was looking through a magazine, waiting to make funeral arrangements, when I came across an article. It was about biodegradable urns or something like that. I thought it was a great idea at the time, and the timing, well..."

"You thought it was an omen," the doc interrupted.

"Yeah, that's it, an omen. You see, we had our son cremated and placed his ashes in this urn. Then we planted the urn in our backyard. It grew into this enormous tree in a matter of a few short years. It was strictly to remember him by. He loved nature."

"Oh, well, I wasn't expecting that," the doc said as he looked at his watch. The session was now running over. He jotted down a few more notes and searched around in his desk drawer. He sorted through some business cards and handed one to Nate. "Here's the card of a friend of mine. She specializes in what your problem may be."

"Which is?"

"I'm sorry, I'm not qualified to say. That's way above

my pay grade. Give her a call."

"You have a doctorate degree and it's above your pay grade? Who is this?" Nate shakes the business card in front of the doc's face.

"Just a figure of speech, if you must know, she specializes in the spirit world."

"You're sending us to a damn fortune teller?" asked Nate.

"No, no, of course not, most of them are fake and just after your money. Have you heard of wood spirits?" The doc looks to both Nathan and Brandy for a response.

"Well, yes, aren't they folklore?" responded Brandy.

"Some people think so, others do not, which is why you must call my friend. Trust me, you'll be glad you did."

Brandy took the card from Nate and thanked the doctor for his time. Nathan, on the other hand, had heard more than enough, and was already out the door and halfway to the car.

Not much was said during the car ride home. Brandy could tell Nate was fuming inside and she didn't want to add fuel to the fire. He kept rambling on, on how much of his hard-earned money was wasted on that quack today, and something about an hour of his life that he could never get back.

Brandy, on the other hand, had much more of an open mind and was always intrigued by the idea of the paranormal world.

•••

CHAPTER 12

The next morning Nate was flagged down while walking by his boss's office.

"Nathan!" he summoned, "Can you come into my office, please?"

"Sure, what's up boss?"

"Please," he motioned to shut the door. "Sit down."

"Doing monthly evaluations early, are ya? Going on vacation?" asked Nate.

"No, nothing like that, Nate. This is actually a personal meeting, off the books, let's say."

"Oh, sounds serious. Did I do something?"

"No, I just wanted you to know that I received a letter from your neighbor. Seems his son overheard your daughter talking about a tree in your backyard, an ash tree. Is this true?"

Nate looked puzzled.

"Do you have an ash tree in your yard, Nate?" his boss, Stan questioned again. "You know, they are banned in this city. It will have to come down if you do."

Nate felt nauseous, and wondered to himself why so much attention was on the tree lately. "To be honest, sir, I don't know what kind of tree it is. A tree is a tree to me," he finally replied.

"Well, if it is, I'm sure you are well aware of what could happen. I'm going to bury this complaint in a mountain of paperwork for now, but if we receive anymore complaints, an investigation will have to be launched."

"I understand, sir. Thanks for bringing it to my attention. I honestly don't know what tree he's talking about, but if it's the one I'm thinking," he paused, "well, that tree means a lot to us, sir, so hopefully it's not an ash, but I'll be checking in to it."

"Great, and by the way, Nate, you're doing great with your position. You'll be receiving a raise in your next check." The mayor looked out his window into the open office floor plan. "There are people watching, so let's just consider this your monthly evaluation, early."

Nate stood up and shook Stan's hand. "Thank you so much, sir. And, thanks for this meeting. I really appreciate it."

The rest of Nate's day was filled with grief, mostly put

on by his own doings. He couldn't stop thinking about that tree and what it would do to the family if something were to happen to it. "Damned Emerald Ash Borers, anyway," he said to himself as he frantically searched online for photos of ash trees. "Hell, I don't know. It could be. A tree's a tree." It was time to go. He clicked his monitor off and headed for home.

When he got home he went around to the backyard. It was fall, but all the leaves were gone, and had already been raked to the roadside for pick up the week before. There were a few leaves scattered here and there, but what tree they came from, he hadn't a clue. They could have been from the neighbor's tree two blocks away, for all he knew. The wind had been blowing pretty hard lately.

Megan, as usual, was out playing under the tree. She was positioning a gnome door at the trunk of the tree, just so.

"What are you doing, Megan?" Nate asked.

"Just playing. Charlie the gnome wants to live in this tree, with Ash. He'll keep him company."

"Oh, I see. Well, tell Charlie I said 'hello'."

"He's right over there, Dad. You can tell him yourself, he's listening, you know."

Nate turned to go inside the slider. He greeted Charlie before going in. "Good day to you, Charlie."

"Talking to garden gnomes now, Nate?" Brandy inquired.

"Oh, hi, I didn't see you there. Yup, Megan has quite

the imagination, doesn't she? Close the door. We need to talk," he said nonchalantly, while walking past.

Brandy slid the door shut. "Okay, about what?"

"Do you happen to know what kind of tree that is, by any chance?"

"No, you know I don't know one tree from another. We've had this discussion."

"Well, when you ordered the urn, did it say on the package?"

"Maybe, but that was almost ten years ago, Nate. Why, what's gong on?"

"It may be nothing, but I got pulled aside at work today. It seems that our wonderful neighbor complained that a tree in our backyard may be an ash tree, and wants it cut down."

"CUT DOWN! WHAT? Over my dead body," yelled Brandy.

"It's a city ordinance. We won't have a choice if the neighbor pushes it."

"We'll see about that, won't we? How do we find out, we need to be prepared?"

"Can you find where you purchased the urn from?" Nathan asked.

"I'll do some checking, but that was a time in our lives that was pretty chaotic, to say the least."

"Yes, I know. Do what you can, will ya?"

"You bet I will. GRRRRR," Brandy growled. "Always something."

•••

CHAPTER 13

The next day while Megan was at school and Nate at work, Brandy parallel-parked in front of a door that listed several services. She read through each one as she approached. "Psychic, Palm Reading, Tarot Cards, Fortune Telling. "He *did* sent me to a fortuneteller. Damn him," she grumbled under her breath.

Pausing at the door for a moment, she peered down at her purse, then at her watch, as if she were trying to come up with an excuse not to keep the appointment she'd made. She grabbed the business card the therapist had given her and confirmed the address printed on the awning above the door.

"Yep, this is the right place. Here goes nothing," she said, taking a deep breath and walking in the door.

Bells chimed overhead as the door slowly swung open. A gypsy-clad, questionable-looking person revealed herself from behind a beaded drape that was surely from the 1960s. She greeted Brandy.

"Hello, come on in. My name is Peggy. You must be?"

"Bran..."

"Brandy, of course. You look like a Brandy. How are ya?"

Right away, with brows raised, Brandy envisioned a man, probably stationed somewhere in the Ukraine, with a Russian accent, calling himself Peggy as he answered the phone for USA Prime Credit. She chuckled as she tried to erase that vision from her mind.

"I said something funny, yes?" Peggy asked, with a ka-ching from her finger cymbals.

"No, no, I'm sorry. My mind was temporarily somewhere else, that's all. Hello," Brandy replied nervously with a nod of her head.

"Oh, you are nervous, aren't you? Please relax. I don't bite. Nibble maybe, but never bite." The gypsy got no response to her joke. "Alrighty then. Lighten up—that was a funny, and you didn't even quiver a lip. What gives?"

"My first time, that's all."

"Oh, I see. A gypsy virgin." The gypsy took a seat on the other side of the crystal ball. She noticed Brandy staring into it. "What do you see?" she asked.

"See? Oh." Brandy looked a little deeper inside. "Um, I'm afraid I don't see anything. Is it on?" She looked for a switch.

The gypsy stared at her kind of funny. "Seriously? Here,

let me take care of that. It's just for show. Some people like the full effect, and I aim to please. I do have to make a living, you know." She picked up the crystal ball and carried it to the back room behind the beaded curtain. When she returned, Brandy was leaving, already halfway out the door.

The gypsy cleared her throat, stopping Brandy in her tracks. "Something I said?"

She was caught. *Think, Brandy, think.* "No, no, I'm just chilled. I was going to get my sweater." That was the best she could do on such short notice.

"Oh, here, have mine. I don't need it anyway. It must be 80 degrees in here." The gypsy took her shawl off and wrapped it around Brandy's shoulders. *Maybe get some meat on them bones of yours and you wouldn't be cold.* "Please, sit." She motioned to the couch before her and continued on in a slightly deeper tone. "That's better. Sorry, I may have come on a bit strong. I didn't mean to make you nervous. Seriously, don't ask me how I know, but you're not the type who would normally visit a fortuneteller, are you? What brings you here?"

Brandy took a deep breath and wondered just how many personalities this woman actually had. "You were recommended by our therapist."

"Ron? Ron Higgins?"

"Yes, Dr. Higgins, that's right. Why?"

"Oh Ron and I go way back. The things he and I use to get away with behind his wife's back." The gypsy giggled, then quickly recovered covering her mouth in surprise. "Did I just say that out loud?"

The gypsy turned her back and took a flask from her deep pocket and took a swig.

Brandy chuckled. "Don't worry, mum's the word."

"Okay, before you go on, would you like a glass of water?"

"Please, and thank you."

The gypsy left the room, pushing the row of beads aside and returning with two bottles of water. After handing one to Brandy, she took out her flask and filled it up.

Brandy looked on with a funny, confused look on her face. "Thanks," she added.

"Oh, it's just water. It goes with the costume. It's all in the presentation. I couldn't come out here dressed like this with a bottle of Aquafina, now could I? It just wouldn't fit. They would think I was a fake right away. You thought I was drinking, didn't you?" Brandy nodded. "Sorry, gave that up 12 years ago. Just water now. Not even a drop of soda anymore."

Brandy started to wonder if they were ever going to talk about what she came here for.

"Why, of course, let's get started," the Gypsy said.

Did she just read my mind? Brandy wondered.

"I sure did. One of the many things that I do." That caught Brandy's attention. "So, let me guess, you're married?"

"Okay, that wasn't hard. I'm wearing a ring," Brandy

interjected.

"Sorry, that wasn't my intention. I was just guessing that your husband is the skeptical one, which is why he isn't here with you."

"Yes, you could say that."

"And you are more open-minded? Or, are you just desperate for answers?"

"Both, actually, but I do have more of an open mind than my husband. Probably more than most people."

"Great, then you believe in ghosts? And the supernatural?"

"Let's just say I don't *not* believe."

"Are you a politician?" she asked.

"No, why?"

"Not important. Let's get on with this. I want you to just relax and think of the biggest issue you have right now. The one thing that, if nothing else comes out of this meeting of ours, you will be satisfied."

Brandy laid back on the couch and closed her eyes.

"Just think of nothing else but the biggest reason why you came here. Be specific."

The gypsy held Brandy's hand and closed her own eyes as well. A minute passed. "Okay, you can open your eyes now." The gypsy helped Brandy up.

"Well?"

The gypsy took in a deep breath from her long e-cig and closed her eyes, slowly releasing the vapor into the air.

Brandy tilted her head as she watched, confused. *She's a modern-day gypsy, smoking an e-cig.*

The gypsy shook her head with her fingers at her temples, as if she had a headache. "Lady... Brandy, I mean. Yes, it's an e-cig. I stopped smoking when I gave up booze, all right? I was a mess back then. Now can you stop thinking about it?"

"I'll try." *She read my mind. She couldn't possibly know that was what I was thinking,* Brandy thought, as smirk crept across the gypsy's face.

"I asked you to think of one thing and one thing only, but I got two images flashing before me while you were lying on the couch. The first image was disturbing, and so was the other."

"Oh, well what did you see?" asked Brandy.

"The first image was of a boy, about twelve years of age, sitting on top of his bunk bed with a rope tied around his neck. Then it flashed over from his bedroom to a large tree."

Brandy gasped and covered her mouth with her hands.

"Brandy, did a boy hang himself in a tree in your backyard?"

Brandy shook her head no. She couldn't believe her ears. She couldn't believe how close the gypsy was.

"Tell me about the boy and his relationship to the tree

then, Brandy."

"The boy was my son," Brandy's eyes already starting to tear up. "He was twelve when he committed suicide in his room. He was bullied, and he couldn't take it anymore."

"Oh, I'm so sorry to hear that, but why do I have a vivid picture of a tree, then? Where does that come into play?

Brandy tried to swallow the lump that formed in her throat. She couldn't believe what she was about to say. "Our boy was cremated, and to make a long story short, I placed the ashes in a special urn, a biodegradable urn. Seeds were mixed in with the ashes, and we buried it out in the backyard. It wasn't long before a tree grew from it. Over the years, it grew to this enormous size. We wanted something special to remember our son, Ashton, by."

The gypsy turned and reached into a cabinet, taking out two glasses. She then grabbed a bottle of whisky and poured a couple of drinks. She drank one, then offered the other to Brandy. "Oh, no, no thanks," Brandy responded, so the gypsy downed that one as well.

"But, I thought..."

"I've been known to fall off the wagon at times. Usually during times like this."

"Oh, so where do we go from here?"

"Go? Well, um, have you ever heard of tree spirits, Brandy?"

"Yeah, we've heard of them."

DAN WALTZ

"We? Did someone else come in when I wasn't looking?" The gypsy looked around.

Are you for real? Brandy thought to herself.

"As real as they come, Brandy."

Brandy's eyes got big. *She did it again!* She didn't want to think anymore, but her brain wouldn't stop. It was in overdrive.

•••

CHAPTER 14

One day, while Nate was away and Brandy was enjoying her favorite soap opera, Megan was out at the tree looking for Ash. The tree was wet from rain, and Ash was nowhere to be seen. She called out for him but received no reply. She was sad and missed him, but had an idea.

Megan quickly ran to the kitchen and grabbed a paring knife from the kitchen drawer. She then walked up to the tree and went to work. Into the bark of the tree, she started to carve a heart-shaped tattoo that she had drawn in her sketchpad. The knife glided through the wet bark with ease, and she hoped that since Ash was gone that he wouldn't feel a thing. *The tattoo should be painless.* After she carved the heart shape in the bark of the tree, she painted inside the grooves with her mom's red fingernail polish. She stepped back to admire her work, and she loved it. *Now Ash will always know he is loved*, she thought.

Just as she finished, a raven landed on a branch above

her. It called out several times as the sun began to show itself from behind the clouds. It wasn't long before the tree bark was dry again, and as soon as it was, Ash reappeared. He looked over at the heart from the corner of his right eye, and a drop of sap appeared, like a tear, where his left eye should have been.

Megan was so fascinated by the large black bird that when she was done carving the heart she ran inside and read as many myths and legends about ravens that she could find. One in particular, she was quite fond of. The legend said, *Because ravens fly so high toward the heavens, they can take prayers from the people on Earth and deliver them to loved ones in Heaven and, in turn, also bring back messages to us below.* This brought Megan much peace and wonder as she drifted off to sleep.

When Megan returned, so did the misty rain. The Raven was still up on the branch bobbing his head.

"Well, hi there!" Meg said, looking up in the tree where the raven had landed. The large black bird lifted his head and made a squawking sound almost as if replying back.

Startled by the loud squawk, Meg regained composure, then cupped her ear with her hand. She heard a faint voice in her head, and thought it could be Ash. It didn't take long for her to determine that it wasn't. This was clearly a different voice, but whose? She looked around and found no one, but the voice repeated louder and louder until it knew that Megan was giving it her full attention.

This voice was speaking in riddles and rhymes and was hard to understand, especially for such a little girl.

The sky will darken,
the wind shall sail.
debris will break,
let fall prevail.

The tree limbs loosen,
the leaves take flight,
the bark shall crumble,
worse than the bite.

They wiggle, they waggle,
they fly, they fall,
where they land,
it's not our call.

They hit the house,
The glass will break,
if not careful,
man has same fate.

Power loss,

darkness falls,

shadows long,

shadows tall.

Ash, oh Ash, you will call.

Three months, he shall fall.

Megan listened intently to the message in rhyme while constantly scanning the area in wonder. She saw nothing out of the ordinary, except for that strange black raven perched above her head. "Was that you?" she asked.

The raven bobbed its head a few times, as if answering, before taking flight, disappearing in the foggy mist.

A loud crack of thunder awoke Megan from her deep sleep. She gasped for air then sat up in bed dazed, but only for a moment. More thunder roused her attention. Fully awake, she grabbed her notepad and wrote down everything she could remember about her dream before she forgot, but her memory was cloudy and the storm was building.

The wind whipped the rain against the house so hard you couldn't hear yourself think, and there were weather warnings posted everywhere.

Meg lay in her bed, listening to the storm crash down on the roof. Lightning lit up the sky, filling her room with bright light, followed by dark shadows and the roar of thunder like a freight train passing through. Over and over, she thought about what the raven said in her dream.

"This is what it meant. *The storm. Three months he will fall.* It was a warning about the storm." As lightning cracked and webbed its way across the sky again and again, Megan reflexively threw her blankets over her head. Under the covers, she hid.

•••

CHAPTER 15

Rain whipped through the air in sheets, slashing hard against the windowpanes. The fake shutters banged loudly against the siding as tree branches brushed up against the house, scraping back and forth like nails on a chalkboard.

Megan couldn't take it any longer. She bolted from her bed and ran down the hall, stopping at the bottom of the stairs. She looked up to complete darkness until lightning struck again, lighting her path. She advanced seven steps, then awaited another strike. It wasn't long before she proceeded up six more steps. In another five, she would reach the top. Another bolt of lightning crashed down, sending Megan to the top of the stairs. She now stood in the doorway of her mom and dad's bedroom. With a weak whimper, she called out for her mom, but the sound was drowned out by the rolling roar of thunder. Another great boom forced her to jump forward in complete darkness. She was afraid to go any farther in the dark. More lightning lit her path, and she ran to her parents' bedside. Another burst of thunder sent her jumping into the bed between them.

"Mom!" she yelled over the thunder's roar in her ear. Brandy instantly jumped to her feet at the sound of her daughter's voice. She was practically out the door when the room lit up again. She looked back and saw a small-framed, silhouetted image sitting up in her bed.

"Meg?" she questioned. "What's wrong, honey?" Just then, the streetlights, nightlights, and electric appliances all went dark.

Feeling safe and sound between her parents, it didn't take long for Megan to fall asleep. But a few minutes later, a bolt of lightning hit hard and nearby; thunder immediately followed. Shortly after that, something came crashing down on the roof, but Nate kept on sleeping. It wasn't until the sound of shattering glass that Nate woke from his sound sleep. He could sleep through almost anything.

"What's going on?" he mumbled, half asleep.

"Just a storm, dear. Megan joined us. She got scared."

"Oh, all right. Um, can she..."

"It's all right, she's asleep."

"I'll grab some flashlights." He swung his legs over the bed and wrapped himself in a robe.

Lightning struck again, followed immediately by a clap of thunder. It rumbled and shook the house like a quake.

"Wow, that was close." Nathan jumped, returning with

the flashlights on. "Power's out."

"It's been out."

"Something hit the roof earlier," said Brandy

"All right. I better have a look."

"Careful, I heard glass."

The flashlight he was holding went out. He smacked it hard against his palm and it came back to life. Nate handed it to Brandy and had to do the same with the other for himself.

"I'll be out back."

"Careful."

"I will, dear." Nate's flashlight went out again. "Dang these things!" he said, smacking it twice against his hip like a tambourine. Once again, there was light. He headed toward the kitchen and paused near the sliding glass door for a second as he watched the wind whip the tree branches back and forth. He was amazed that they still hung on. Obviously some did not, as more branches fell to the roof.

Wind gusts sent sheets of rain slashing hard against the glass door like large waves against a ship. Nathan sat at the table and watched, wishing he had a hot cup of coffee. Then he remembered the power was out and settled for a cold soda. The storm became quite the light show when Nate decided it would be best to get the girls into the basement for cover.

Nathan carried Megan, who was half asleep, down the stairs with a flashlight clenched between his teeth to light the way. Brandy followed close behind with an armload of pillows and blankets, and her flashlight. Thunder clapped overhead, over and over again, now muffled behind the closed doors of their underground refuge.

While Brandy and Megan lay comfortably on the couch in the basement, Nate headed back upstairs for more supplies and to check again for damage. He finished his soda at the kitchen table while watching the storm build even stronger. He couldn't wait any longer. He grabbed an umbrella and stepped outside on the deck.

Nate's umbrella quickly inverted in his hand, extending his arm to full length; he did his best to keep hold. There was an incredible updraft as dime-size hail began to fall, peppering him and quickly covering the ground. Knowing the dangers that could follow, Nate hurried back inside and raced down the stairs, slamming the door behind. He ordered Brandy to get Megan and herself under the pool table for cover. Just being downstairs no longer seemed enough.

Startled, they heard more breaking glass, shattering on the floor above their heads. Brandy jumped, hitting her head on the underside of the pool table.

Twenty minutes later, the storm subsided, leaving behind a greenish-grey sky and a light drizzle of rain. Nate ran outside to check for damage. The tree out back had shed quite a few limbs, bombarding the roof with branches and twigs. But Nate found no signs of any real damage, with the exception of one branch sticking through the small kitchen window above the sink. All in all, the damage was far less than what he'd expected. Later, they found out that a couple of houses down the road were completely demolished by two confirmed tornados.

Brandy came walking through the basement door. "Everything all right?" she asked.

"Just fine, nothing serious. It looks like the worst of it has passed. Why don't you get Megan and head back to bed?"

"I'm up now. Coffee?"

"Sorry, dear, no power. Pop?"

She nodded. "I'll grab some candles and cookies."

•••

CHAPTER 16

Stan stood at the podium and greeted the crowd at the town hall meeting. "Thank you all for coming." He paused, waiting for their full attention. Silence filled the room. "We have a couple of things to discuss tonight, so, please, let's get started.

"First on the slate is Taylor's hardware store. I'm sorry, but it looks like your parking permit has been denied. The committee felt it's too close to the alley and could cause a traffic hazard." A hand immediately raised in the audience. "Sir?"

"Bob Taylor, Taylor Hardware. I don't understand. Jay's Pizza has identical parking and has no issues. What gives?"

"Sorry, Bob. It went to a vote and was voted down. You're welcome to resubmit your proposal and maybe include pictures and measurements next time. Maybe they just didn't have enough information."

"You bet I will. This is ridiculous. Another wasted month," Bob replied. He stood and left the room in disgust.

"Okay, next, the ash tree crisis. As you all know, ash trees are banned in this city and must be cut down and properly destroyed. We don't want an infiltration of the Emerald Ash Borer here. We ask the public to please comply. Many of you have taken care of this already, and we do appreciate the cooperation. If residents come forward and report their trees to the city by the 15th of this month, the city will take care of it for you at the city's reduced rate, which, I don't mind saying, is a pretty good savings. This alone should prompt action, so please comply. If cited after the 15th, no discount will be available, and the residents will be given 30 days to take care of it themselves. Keep in mind that there are limited local tree services in our county, and they may get backed up. If trees still stand after the 30 days, you'll be fined a maximum of $50 per day, per tree, until they are taken care of. I know this sounds stiff, but we do not want to end up like our neighboring county. If you plainly don't have the funds at this time, please do yourself a favor and contact my office by the 15th, and we will try to make arrangements for you. We could break it down into a simple payment structure and tack a percentage onto your water bill each month. Again, after the 15th, there will be no assistance available for the public. You will be on your own." The mayor took a long drink of water.

"With that said, it has been brought to my attention that a certain city employee is harboring one of these trees.

Please be advised, this will be taken care of shortly. The employee has been notified of the issue and has begun talks on how to best handle it. It is a complicated matter. For right now, the employee's name will be held in confidentiality. If rumors are started and heard, just know that it is being taken care of." There was a pause to look over some paperwork. "It appears that is all I have for this evening. Do we have any questions or concerns from the floor?"

A couple of people raised their hands. "Miss?" the mayor selected.

"Is the city going to be decorating the street lamp posts again this year for the holidays? That was so pretty last year."

"Yes, yes I do believe that is budgeted." The mayor looked away to a man in the back. He nodded, "sir, in the back?"

"They are going to be cutting that tree down, aren't they? It's right next door to my property, and I want it taken care of promptly. I had to cut mine down and it cost me $1,400 out of my own damn pocket. Why is it now negotiable? Cut it down and send him the bill."

"It's being taken care of, sir. There are a few complications that need to be addressed first."

"Complications? It's a damn ash tree with bugs. What kind of complications could there be?"

"Sir, it can't be discussed at this time. For the last time, it's being handled. Anyone else?" Irritated, he saw no other hands in the air, but he only glanced up for a split second, with a blind eye. "Good, thank you all for coming. This meeting is now adjourned."

A lot of chatter could be heard from the crowd as they filtered out the door to go home. Stan listened in on as much as he could hear.

"Fifty dollars a day! You've got to be kidding me."

"Yeah, that's bullshit. Someone's making the bucks, that's for sure."

"Glad I don't have any of them ash trees."

"What the hell does that bug do to cause all of this?"

"Just another way for our city government to get more of our damn money, that's all."

"Cut it down, Mayor. Cut it down!" This came from Jim Hernandez, Nate's next-door neighbor, yelling as he closed the door behind him.

"Man, Nathan must have pissed in that man's Cheerios a time or two. He had revenge in his voice," the mayor said to himself as he left the floor.

Nate's phone buzzed and danced across the kitchen table as a text message came through. Nate picked it up. It was his boss, the mayor. "See me in my office first thing," it read.

"Oh boy, that can't be good," Nate said.

"What? Who was that?" Brandy asked.

"It was my boss. He wants to talk to me first thing tomorrow."

"Oh, what about?"

"I have a feeling it's about the tree. They had a town meeting tonight."

"Meeting? You didn't go?"

"I was told that it might be in my best interest to sit this one out. He was expecting something to hit the fan. Looks like it did."

"Great, that's just great."

"Any luck finding out any information regarding the tree?"

"No, but I'll keep looking."

"Thanks, honey. We'll get through this, you know?"

"Yeah, we always do," Brandy answered back.

One leg, followed slowly by the other, swung wide over the coffee table before dropping down to the floor. Nate felt exhausted as he dragged himself off the couch the next morning. He didn't sleep well at all and moved to the couch in the middle of the night so he wouldn't disturb Brandy. His mind couldn't release the worry over the meeting he was about to have with his boss.

While getting ready for work, he dreaded going in and tried to come up with excuses to stay home. Not one legitimate idea came to mind, so he left for work without even saying goodbye to his family. He was in no mood for consoling words, so he let Brandy sleep.

"Nate, please come in. Sit down," Stan greeted, shutting the door behind him.

"Oh boy, here we go," Nate nervously replied under his breath.

"How's the family, Nate?"

Oh good, there's nothing better than a little small talk first, he thought to himself. "Good, Stan. Listen, I'm not much into small talk. I got little to no sleep last night. Can you just cut to the chase and tell me what this is all about? I assume it's about the town meeting last night."

"Sure, Nate. We can do that. The meeting didn't go so hot. Your neighbor is a real piece of work."

"Yeah, I know."

"Did you two have a falling out or something?"

"No, Stan, we just never got along from day one. He still holds a grudge for me putting his son in jail. Now look at the other one. He's headed there too."

"Well, that's too bad," Stan said. "I've given your situation a great deal of thought, Nate."

"And?"

"Well, people are asking questions, and there are rumors flying around here about me helping you keep the tree."

"Rumors? How?"

"Not sure how, but they are out there, for sure. I've bought you a little time, Nate. You have 'til spring to determine the species of the tree you have, but I sure hope after all this, it's not an ash. After that, I can't help you. In fact, the council has forced my hand, Nate."

"Forced your hand? What does that mean, exactly?"

"It means I have to put you on administrative leave without pay until then."

"What?" Nate stared at the mayor in disbelief. Stan shook his head in return. "I see. Well, I kind of had the feeling it was headed in a bad way, so it's really no surprise to me."

"You're a good employee, Nate. I'll bring you back in the spring, I promise. Let this thing blow over, and we'll start anew then."

Nathan had nothing more to say. He hung his head low as he left the mayor's office, worried about losing the house as well as the tree. "I lose either way," he mumbled to himself.

Back to the park, Nathan thought sarcastically, triggering a list of things that raced through his mind. *Relocate? Out of the question.* He could never convince the family to move away from Ash. *We should have thought this through a little better than we did. When Brandy bought that urn, we all thought it was a great idea but never dreamed that it would tether us to a house we can't afford.*

Losing Ash the first time was hard enough. Now they faced the possibility of abandoning him to live in someone else's backyard.

How do you say goodbye to a family tree? Nate thought, chuckling to himself at the pun.

Beeeeeeeeeep! Beeep! Beeeeeeep! Beeep! The car behind Nate's blasted its horn as Nate daydreamed, stationary at a green light on his way home. Nate didn't even respond until the third long beep. Breaking his train of thought, he jumped in his seat and stepped on the gas.

•••

CHAPTER 17

"Hello, Mayor," Jim, Nate's neighbor, said as he walked up to him at the grocery store.

Stan knew that voice in an instant, and it startled him. He turned, cringed, and nodded with a smile as he continued on his way, just like any good politician would before election year.

"What's your hurry? No time for a taxpaying citizen?"

"I heard enough from you at last night's meeting, Mr. Hernandez. If you have something more to say, call my office and make an appointment, or I'll cite you for harassment."

"Now, Mayor, that's no way to talk. I just want what should be done, and if it ain't done, I'll take care of it myself, and you can forget elections next year."

"Are you threatening me, Jim?"

"No sir, I'm promising you." Jim looked down into the mayor's grocery cart. "Enjoy your donuts, Mayor." He turned and left before Stan could respond.

Stan, a little shaken up, pulled a hankie from his pocket to wipe his brow. "Asshole," he whispered as he carried on with his shopping.

Three aisles over, in the bread aisle, he ran into his brother-in-law, Gabe.

"Hey, Gabe. Boy, am I glad I ran into you."

"What's up, boss?"

"I just ran into Jim Hernandez, Renard's neighbor."

"Yeah, I saw you over there talking to him."

"Yeah, well, he's nothing but trouble. I'm afraid he's going to do something crazy. He's insane."

"Yeah? Like what?"

"I don't know. He's threatening my re-election if I don't cut that damn tree down."

"Really."

"We have to do something, and quick."

"Two hours, Stan. That's all I need, and it will all go away."

Stan didn't reply.

"Think about it. I can make it happen."

"Without a trace?" Stan asked.

"Without a trace."

This was on Stan's mind the rest of the day, the

evening, and throughout the night. He hardly slept, and he let it continue on the next morning over coffee and donuts, which brought up vivid memories of the conversation again. *Enjoy your donuts — enjoy your donuts — it could be all over in two hours' time. Two hours' time — time — another term — term — donut.*

Stan had to make the decision. *I can make it happen — two hours.* The words just repeated in his head. He took another sip of coffee, then whipped the rest of his donut into the trash, irritated with his thoughts.

•••

CHAPTER 18

"You have to help us," Nate said to the rather distinguished-looking attorney sitting across the conference table. Nate took one look at him and wondered what he and Brandy were doing there. They couldn't even afford the Italian suit the lawyer was wearing. Stacks of papers were splayed across the table before attorney, as he sat in front of rows of perfectly placed books, displayed on the bookshelves that stretched across the back of the room. Law books, and not a one an inch out of place.

"I will certainly try. What do you have?" the attorney dryly questioned, looking over his round spectacles. "Please, start at the beginning."

The beginning? Of course, he's paid by the hour, Nate thought as he quickly did the numbers in his head. "About ten years ago, our son died. He was a sweet boy, born with a cleft lip and no palate. Because of his deformities, he was teased a lot—bullied practically his whole life. He eventually couldn't take it anymore, so he ended it."

"Oh my, I'm so sorry, but I'm not that kind of attorney."

"No, there's more."

The lawyer nodded to continue. "It's your money."

"Well, we wanted something special to remember him by. You know, so he can live on. So Brandy here," Nate motioned to his wife, "came across an article about a living urn."

"Living urn?"

"Yes, you put cremated ashes in the urn and plant it in the ground with the seeds of a tree or plant, and it uses the ashes to grow. Well, ten years later, the city wants us to cut the tree down, because they think it's an ash tree."

"Well is it? Ash trees are illegal in this city. I had to remove one myself a month ago."

"That's the thing. We don't know, but even if it is, isn't there some kind of protection we can get to protect our son's burial site? Even Indian burial grounds have rights, do they not?"

"Well, yes, yes they do, but I would have to look into this. What we could do for now is start a case while we do a little research. That will stop any harassment by the city until this case is settled by trial. In the meantime, I'll do some research and try to build a case."

"Great, thank you! Do you think we have a case?"

"Until I look further into it, I don't know."

"All right. Well, what do we have to do?"

"I have to warn you. An unknown case like this can get expensive. I will need a retainer of $15,000."

"Fifteen thousand dollars! Are you kidding me?"

"I'm afraid not. This is going to take an enormous amount of research; it will probably go higher, but that will get me started."

"Started? Thanks, but we'll have to think about it and get back to you. To be honest, we don't have that kind of money."

"I see. Well, give it some thought. If it's important enough to you, you'll find a way." The lawyer looked at his watch and scribbled something on a piece a paper and handed it to them. "You can pay this at the counter. Thank you for coming in." It was a bill for half an hour of his time.

Nate noticed Brandy's teary eyes before she looked away, trying to hide them. He then looked at the bill. It was for $150. He turned to ask a final question. "Just where do average people like us find the money they don't have to pay for legal help?"

The attorney answered, "There are many avenues. They take out a loan, borrow from family, or take out a second mortgage on their house. Some will even load up their credit cards, but that's not recommended. It all depends on just how important the issue is."

"I see. Well, thank you." Nathan paid the bill at the counter before leaving and sarcastically mentioned that he would never be able to come up with the retainer.

The receptionist openly offered one more way to raise

the money the attorney hadn't mentioned. "My boyfriend raised $50,000 with a Kickstarter campaign online. He used the money for some trip he needed or wanted to take for research for his new book. If your cause is worthy enough, there are people out there on the web willing to help. I apologize for listening in on your case, but you should give it a try. It sounded like a worthy enough cause to me."

"Thank you. We certainly will," Nate replied. "Did you hear that Brandy?"

•••

CHAPTER 19

"Nathan, can we talk?"

"Sure, hon. What's on your mind?"

"Well, I knew you wouldn't go, so I went without you. Don't be mad."

"Mad? About what? Where did you go?"

"I was desperate for answers, so I went to see the gypsy that the therapist recommended."

"Oh!"

"Are you mad?"

"Don't be silly. How was it?" He shrugged, hoping for some answers himself.

"It was really a fascinating experience, Nate. You should have come. She was really a mind reader."

"Oh? Go on," he chuckled.

"She said that we have a tree spirit and that it's Ashton.

Megan has formed a bond with him and probably knows more about Ashton than we think. She said that their level of communication is far greater than yours and mine."

"So Megan's a Doctor Doolittle, but with trees. What do you call it, 'a tree whisperer,' so to speak?"

"There you go again. Always making fun."

"No, no, honey, I'm just trying to understand. It was a question, that's all."

"Yeah, well, kind of, but only with that tree, not others."

"Is she for real?" Brandy looked at Nate like she didn't understand the question. "The gypsy. Is she for real?"

"Well, I have to admit, Nate, she's a bit different, but she's authentic."

"Authentic? What does that mean? Sounds old."

"Not 'antique,' silly," she chuckled. "She knew a lot of things without me telling her. It was no trick, Nate. It was quite eerie. She truly believes that the tree grew up from Ashton's spirit. In a sense, the tree *is* Ashton, and that's why there is such a bond between the two."

"Oh, come on. You actually believe that crap?"

Brandy used the same response she gave the gypsy. "I don't *not* believe it, Nate."

"What is that supposed to mean? You 'don't not' believe? I mean, what kind of political answer is that? And why hasn't Ashton tried to contact us? Why her? Why

Megan? She's just a little girl."

"I asked the same thing, and that's exactly why."

"What?"

"It's because she's just a little girl. Our minds are set in our ways, filled with negative thoughts, and can'ts. We have the 'have to see it to believe it' mentality. When you're a kid, your imagination runs wild, in overdrive. You believe in everything, and you believe everything you hear."

"You're telling me!"

"Children are more into believing until proven otherwise. Kids live their lives in a dreamland. They believe everything until the big bad world falls down on them."

"I don't know, hon. This is..." Nate scratched the back of his head.

"According to the gypsy, a tree spirit's spirit is as meek as its host, and we all know Ashton's spirit was beaten, so it's understandable why he never reached out to us. He didn't want to fail. He wasn't strong enough to override our defenses, so he reached out to Megan instead." She paused. "She also told me one other thing, Nate. She said that Ashton is still around because he wasn't ready to leave. His suicide may have been an accident, like the unfinished letter, Nate. The note he didn't finish."

"Okay, you're starting to freak me out here," Nate said, rubbing the goose bumps from his arms.

Silence fell between Nate and Brandy. Then Nate had

had enough.

"I can't take this anymore!" barked Nate. "I just don't frickin' get it, Brandy."

"Get what?"

"If it's not one thing, it's another."

"With who? What are you talking about, Nate?"

"Last week it was a storm. The week before, it was ants. Before that, bees and birds. Then there was the wind, rain, and fungus. Pretty soon it will be ice and sleet. Now gypsies! Are you kidding me? You act as if you believe all this crap. When will it end? Megan treats that tree like a living, breathing person. She's obsessed with it. It's just a tree! It will weather the storms and bend in the wind, and, by golly, it will shed a few branches and leaves now and then."

"It's also her imaginary friend, Nate. And don't forget it's the only friend she has and cares about."

"The key word there is 'imaginary.' She thinks it's real! That's not healthy."

"I don't see anything wrong with having an imagination, Nate. It's real to her."

"It's as real as a dream. Then you wake up. She needs to come to grips with reality. She's driving me nuts. Speaking of nuts, she was worried about the squirrels making a nest up there."

"Are you saying you don't believe," Nate? "Because I thought you did, I thought you were trying."

"I am. I was. The problem I have with this whole damn thing is that I do, and I don't understand it!"

"Well, I'm just glad you didn't get mad."

•••

CHAPTER 20

"Hi, hon. What are you up to?" asked Nate as he hung up his coat.

"Nate, you're home. Come here. I have something to show you." Nate walked over and looked at the computer screen in front of Brandy. She seemed excited.

"Whatcha got?" Nate asked.

"Look, I started a Kickstarter, and people have already donated."

"Really!" Nathan took a closer look, amazed at what he saw. "Twenty-two hundred dollars, and they don't even know us."

"Yeah! And just within a few hours."

"Wow, that's great, hon! Not to change gears on you, but can you do me a favor and look up tree doctors in the area?"

"Tree doctors? Seriously? There's such a thing?"

"Yeah, or a horticulturist. We need to have someone who knows something about trees, someone able to correctly identify them in the winter. We need to put this thing behind us. Maybe it's not an ash at all."

"Okay, I'll get right on it."

"Thanks, dear. Hopefully somebody with credentials. This may end up in court."

"Let's hope not. We can't afford it." Brandy looked out the window to the backyard. "But we can't afford not to, either." She paused. "Speaking of court, how was it?"

"Looks open-and-shut to me. The parents of the deceased looked like they're doing well, though. I gave them our condolences."

"I hope they lock that kid up and throw away the key. That whole family just disgusts me."

"Me too, hon. The defense is trying to pin it on the school and the bus driver, though. They're making it sound good, but I just don't buy into it."

"What do you mean? What are they saying?"

"They're saying, 'kids will be kids.'"

"Boy, I heard enough of that with Ashton."

"Yeah, I know. They're saying the school district, mainly the driver, just didn't do enough to protect the children. So they want the school to take the rap and not ruin another young man's life."

"Well, they kind of have a point, but..."

"Yeah, I suppose they do. We'll see."

"Should be interesting."

"And thanks for setting up the Kickstarter, Brandy. That looks promising, but hopefully we won't need it."

●●●

CHAPTER 21

It was a long, cold winter. A winter filled with worry and dread. With Nate off work and sky-high heating bills, they barely scraped by and fell behind on a few non-essential bills.

The tree doctor that Brandy found finally came out and examined the tree, but unfortunately could only narrow it down to two different species—one being an ash the other a type of maple. He said he couldn't tell for sure until it produced its fruit, unless he took a DNA sample, which would be costly and take quite a bit of time. By the time the results would be in, spring would have arrived, so they decided to wait it out.

"Dad? Mom?" Megan spoke meekly as she entered the family room where her parents were enjoying a movie together.

"Yes, dear? What is it?" Brandy paused the movie. It was a classic, "The Diary of a Little Girl."

"Something's wrong with Ash," Megan continued.

"What do you mean? Is there something wrong with the tree?" asked Nate.

"Look," Megan handed a tiny leaf to her mom.

"The leaves are covered with them," Megan added.

"Nate, look!" Brandy panicked. "What are those spots? Poison? Do you think Jim would go to that level and poison Ash?"

"I wouldn't put anything past that bastard. He's an angry old man, honey. Seems anger runs in the family."

Nate ran outside to take a look for himself. Sure enough, the tree was loaded with new leaves, and every leaf on the tree was covered with tiny black spots.

"Let's look it up online, Nate. Take a picture of it with your phone and send it to me."

"Okay," Nate answered, not sure what she was up to.

After Brandy received the photo, she saved it to the desktop and uploaded it to the Google image window. Lo and behold, hundreds of images of leaves with black spots filled the screen. Brandy clicked on the image that was the most similar. It took her to a larger photo on an info page.

"You're a flippin' genius," spouted Nate as he stared at the screen. Nate started to read the text. "It says here that it's a fungus that the tree contracted."

"A fungus? Will it be all right?" Brandy asked.

"Hold on." Nate read on. "Here, here it is. Not deadly.

Cure only by fall clean up. Make sure all leaves are raked and discarded in the fall."

Brandy breathed a sigh of relief. "It will be fine, then?"

"Sounds like it." Nate also sighed. "Wait a minute." A light bulb turned on in Nate's head. "It has leaves. The tree has leaves! What kind of tree is it? Go back, go back."

Brandy hit the back arrow on the browser, and there it was, staring them right in the face. The same shape and color. It was only lacking size, which was understandable for new growth.

"It says it's a box elder," said Nate.

"Box elder? Isn't that the bug?" which confused Brandy.

"Yes, it is a bug, but not *the* bug. It's not the Emerald Ash bug. And that's all that matters. It's a box elder, a type of maple, Brandy. It's a maple tree, not an ash. We're good. The tree is safe. Ash is safe."

"But, Nate, look. It kind of looks like this leaf too," Brandy said as she pointed to the computer screen. "And it says here that it's an ash."

"Let me see that." Nate quickly took Brandy's seat and studied the screen. "No, look, honey. Look at the shape. See the notches? I know they're small, but they aren't in the ash leaf at all."

Brandy agreed. The leaf definitely came from a box elder, a maple. Nate grabbed the leaf and ran to the neighbor's house to show the bastard so he'd back off, but no one was at home. Both cars were gone. Disappointed, he ran back home and phoned his boss.

"Mayor Stan here," he answered.

"Stan, it's Nate."

"Nate, how is everything? Everything all right?"

"I need to talk to you right away. I know it's a Saturday, but are you busy?"

"Actually, I was just headed to the office, Nate. I have to run some copies for my wife, on taxpayers' dollars, if you know what I mean. You're welcome to join me. I should be there awhile."

"Great, I'll grab the family and be right there."

"Oh, okay." *Hmmmm, bringing the family. Must be important.* "What's this about, Nate?"

"I'll tell you when I get there." Nate hung the phone up and gathered the family. They drove down to city hall to show Stan their findings.

Nate, Megan, and Brandy exited the car and bee-lined to the front door of City Hall. The door was locked, but Nate noticed Stan's car in its usual spot.

Nate knocked on the glass, but to no avail. No one came to the door. He then tapped on the glass with his ring. The tapping echoed down the hall and cut through anything that got in its way. Stan appeared around the corner a moment later. He was on the phone, cord stretched to its limits. He held one finger up, signaling for them to wait a minute.

The wait was longer than a minute, but eventually Stan came to the door. "Sorry, come on in," he greeted.

Nate introduced his wife and daughter as they headed to Stan's office.

"Well, what's this all about, Nate?" Stan asked.

Nate lifted up the leaf in front of him.

"A leaf?" Stan questioned, knowing perfectly well what it was.

"Not just a leaf, Stan. *The* leaf. Off our tree."

"Oh, well, what do you have?"

"It's a maple, not an ash."

"A maple, huh? I'm no tree expert, but that doesn't look like a maple leaf to me, Nate. In fact, it looks a lot like the leaves on the ash trees we've been cutting down. We've cut down a bunch of them. It's an ash, Nate."

"No it's not. It's not your typical silver maple, like the Canada leaf, but rather a box elder."

"Box elder? Really! It looks like an ash to me."

"No, look. Can I use your computer?" Stan motioned for Nate to take a seat at the computer. "Hon?" Nate, in turn, motioned to Brandy. She quickly looked up the box elder in Google images.

Due to a slow computer and internet connection, it took some time, but Brandy finally was able to pull up some images to convince Stan that it was, in fact, a maple leaf and not an ash. Stan took back his seat at the desk. He combed his fingers through his hair and wiped the sweat beading on his brow. After a long gaze at the clock on the wall, he inhaled, taking in enough air to blow up a balloon. He released it slowly.

Nate noticed more beads of sweat forming on Stan's forehead. "Stan, are you all right?" he asked.

Stan wiped his brow again while pulling some paperwork from a file cabinet across the room. "Yeah, I'm fine." He loosened his tie and opened a window for some air. "Gosh, it's hot in here."

"Can I get you something, Stan? You're not looking so good. Sure you're all right?"

"Yeah, yeah, I'm fine, Nate. Thanks. I feel like a woman going through menopause lately. The hot flashes come and go." He shuffled through some papers. "Listen, Nate. This may take a little bit. Why don't you take the family next door for lunch, on me, and give me about an hour to do this paperwork."

"You're going to do it right now?"

"No time like the present. I have to wait for those copies to run anyway."

"That's awesome! Thanks so much, Stan! Will do," said Nate. "Come on. Let's let him work."

Nate and the family had spent about an hour at the diner when Nate thought he saw Stan's car drive off. He excused himself from the table. "Hon, I'll be back. I just want to check Stan's progress."

"Oh, all right. We're done here, so why don't we all go?" Brandy asked, wondering why Nate wanted to go alone.

"No, really. I'll be back. Order some dessert. I want to talk to him about my job as well. I don't want to put him on the spot in front of you. I'll call you when I know something."

Brandy nodded.

Once out, Nate noticed that Stan's car was indeed gone, and the doors to the city offices were locked. There was a note on the door. Nate grabbed it with a swipe of the wrist. He feared the worst as he read.

Nate, the judge owes me a favor, so I'm going straight to his house to have this signed. Go have some dessert. I'll be right back. Maybe get your job back real soon too. Be glad when this whole thing is behind us. Stan.

Nate breathed a sigh of relief and headed back to the diner with a smile, and just in time. Dessert was served the moment he sat down.

"Good timing. How did it go? I got you a slice of pie," said Brandy.

"Thanks, dear. He wasn't there."

"What? Where did he go?"

"He went to have the papers signed by the judge. The note said he would be right back."

Fifteen minutes later, Nate received a text from his

boss. "Nate, sorry, the judge wasn't home. We'll take care of this first thing Monday. I promise. And bring me the receipt for lunch. I'll take care of that, as well."

Nate hung his head as disappointment crept in.

"Nate? Is everything all right?" Brandy softly inquired.

"Yeah, it's fine. It was Stan. The papers can't be signed until Monday now. The judge wasn't home. Come on, let's go."

Several stops and an hour or so later, they finally pulled into their driveway. As he stepped out of the car, Nate sensed that something was different. The grass in the front yard was trampled, as if it had been driven on, but the tread marks looked more like heavy equipment than a car. Nate's gut churned when his eyes followed the tracks around to the back of the house. He then hesitantly looked up over the garage, as if he knew what to expect. He instantly fell to his knees. What he would usually see was no longer there.

"*No!*" Nate yelled at the top of his lungs, pounding his fists on the ground. His heart sank. Brandy and Megan came running the second they heard his scream. Nathan got to his feet before they got there and took off running around to the backyard. His family followed close behind at a full sprint.

"They took it! They took our son!" Nathan cried as he rounded the corner of the house. He fell to his knees once again as soon as he had a clear view. The tree was gone, cut to the ground, every twig hauled away. All that was left was a stump protruding from the earth eighteen inches.

The family huddled in devastation, eyes beet-red and jaws agape. Tears started to flow down Brandy and Megan's cheeks, while rage burned like bile in the back of Nate's throat.

A moment later, Nathan broke the embrace and marched to the neighbor's house. He banged on the door with everything he had, almost knocking the door off its hinges. But no one answered. He screamed, "Jim! Get your ass out here!" But no one came. He moped back home, constantly looking back over his shoulder in hopes of seeing his neighbor return.

"Nate, look," Brandy said, pointing to Megan.

"I know, dear, I know."

They both watched Megan from afar as she sat all alone on the ground next to Charlie the garden gnome. He stood only two feet from the tree stump. Nate and Brandy, hands held, got up and sat on each sides of her. They held each other until the sun went down.

That evening, Nate and Brandy spent time mourning the death of their son once again. The nine years that had passed didn't seem to make it much easier.

Depression set in on the whole family, hitting Brandy the hardest, just as it had before. This time was slightly different, though. This time, she could share the grief with her daughter, but she handled things differently. Megan went into shock and started to shut down. She stopped doing everything she loved to do—singing, drawing, reading, and writing were now the furthest things from her mind. Her daily logs in her diary came to an abrupt halt, and her schoolwork suffered.

Nate and Brandy felt helpless. There wasn't anything anyone could say or do to make Megan feel better or to make her understand what had happened. They could use a little help in that department themselves.

Nate filed a police report the next morning, not knowing what else to do or even what good it would do. *It won't bring Ash back. What's done is done.* They now needed to learn to cope.

•••

CHAPTER 22

On the way home from filing the police report, Nathan reminisced about earlier days. He thought back to when Megan would spend hours under the tree in the backyard. There she would play with Charlie and talk with Ash for hours on end. He wasn't sure why, but his thoughts ended on the conversation they'd had when Megan found out they use to have a dog named Sparky. He recalled her asking if she could have one too.

In that moment, a sign reading "Humane society" caught his eye. For years he'd driven that route and never once noticed it before.

Nate turned the car around and stopped in for a visit. He looked around and walked past cage after cage of the most sad-looking animals he'd ever seen. They all needed homes, but some appeared to have given up hope and didn't even look at Nate as he walked by. Nate remembered feeling like that himself, during the days he spent at the park after losing his job. People would pass by without even saying hello. Nor did Nate make any effort either. He had felt like an outcast as well, ashamed to be alive. But then there were dogs who eagerly greeted him at the gate, wagging their butts so hard their tails were nothing but a blur. Nate reached in and petted the ones starving for affection.

How would I ever pick? Nate thought. Then it dawned on him that it should be Megan's choice. Nate left the facility sad, but renewed. He felt good about what he was about to suggest to Brandy as soon as he got home.

"How's my little girl?" Nate asked as Megan walked in. "What are you doing?"

"Oh, nothing. Just watching TV, Dad." She hid a notepad behind her back.

"Do you know where your mother is?"

"I think she's just taking a nap."

Nathan walked into their bedroom. "Hi, hon, everything all right?"

Brandy rolled over. "Just tired."

"You rarely take naps, and when you do it's never in here. What really gives?"

"I'm just not sure what to do about Megan. She just has no interest in anything anymore."

"Yeah, I know. It's a gorgeous day out and she's watching television." He paused. "I've been thinking."

"Oh?"

"Yeah. We use to have a dog. How about getting a friend for Megan? Like old times."

"Boy, I don't know, dear. I miss Sparky, but are we ready for that kind of commitment again? Do you think she's ready for the responsibility? It's a lot for a seven-year-old, and you know what happened last time."

"That won't happen again. I fixed that gate last week."

"Sparky's been gone for almost nine years now, Nate."

"Yeah, what's your point? I told you I'd fix it."

Brandy chuckled.

"I really miss that dog." He paused a moment to remember old times. "It was just a thought, hon. You might be right. It may be too early."

●●●

CHAPTER 23

Everyone in Megan's life knew what was wrong, but they just didn't know quite how to approach it. Megan's teachers helplessly watched her grades go downhill. Megan just wasn't the same person anymore.

Brandy's phone rang. She answered, "Hello?" It was early morning, and she wondered who would possibly be calling so early.

"Hello, Brandy?"

"Yes"

"This is Colleen Pratt, Megan's English teacher."

"Hi, Colleen. Megan talks about you all the time. How are you?"

"I'm fine, Brandy. Thanks. It's about your daughter. She's completely shut down. She used to be such an over-achiever in her writing, but she hasn't completed any work in days. Is everything all right?"

Brandy was floored. She had seen a difference in her herself at home, but in school too? Megan had always been a good student. Brandy didn't think that the family's troubles at home would affect Megan at school as well. "Well..." Brandy was at a loss for words and didn't really know how to respond to this. "We have some problems here at home, and it must be carrying over to her schoolwork. I'll talk to her."

"Okay, Brandy. I hope you work through your issues, whatever they may be. She's always been a wonderful student."

"Thanks, Colleen. I appreciate the call."

Not an hour had gone by when the phone rang again.

"Hello, this is Brandy."

"Brandy, this is Mrs. Tartonnie, Megan's math teacher from Centennial Elementary."

Uh, oh. "Yes, what can I do for you?"

"It's about your daughter, Megan."

"And what about her?"

"Today is the fifth day she has fallen asleep during class. Is she getting her rest at home?"

Brandy took a deep breath. "We've had some issues lately, and I didn't realize they were causing a problem at school. I will certainly talk to her."

"Very good, Brandy. I really just wanted you to be aware. She's always been a great kid. I hope you can work things out. If you need any help, we have some great counselors here at the school who would be more than happy to assist."

"Thanks so much for the call."

Brandy had no sooner hung up the phone when it rang again. She didn't want to answer it, but she did. "Brandy here."

"Brandy?"

"Yes…"

"Did I catch you at a good time?"

"Who is this?"

"Centennial's gym teacher. I'm calling about…"

"Megan," Brandy interrupted.

"Yes, that's right. She's been refusing to participate in any of the activities. It's unlike her. She's usually pretty outgoing, but lately something has taken the wind out of her sails. Is everything all right at home?"

"Yes, things are fine. We've had a mishap, and we are trying to deal with things. I had no idea…"

"That's why I'm calling, just to let you know."

"Thanks, I'll talk to her."

"Very well. Take care, Brandy."

After the gym teacher had hung up, Brandy was afraid to hang up herself, but she did, and, just as she'd feared, it rang a fourth time. This time it was Nate.

"Hi, hon. Why was the phone busy for so long? I've

been trying to call you."

"It was the school, Nate."

"Everything okay?"

"We'll talk when you get home, all right Nate?"

"Sure, honey. I was just calling to tell you I'm on my way."

"Great, see you in a bit."

"Love you." The phone went dead.

She hung up again and stared at the phone, waiting for it to ring one more time. She almost dared it to, but it didn't, at least not until she reached to lay it down on the counter. She jumped when it rang and decided to let it go to voicemail. She had heard enough.

Nate walked in the door and found Brandy on the couch, her face in her hands. "Brandy, are you all right?"

She stood and gave Nathan a big hug, then pulled back with teary eyes.

"Hey, hey, hey, what's wrong?" he asked, wiping tears away with his thumbs.

"It's Megan."

"Megan? Where is she? She all right?"

"She's on her way home from school. She's fine, but..."

"But what?"

"I've been on the phone all day with her teachers. Why? How? How are we missing the signs, Nate? How?"

"Signs? What signs? Talk to me. Sit down. Let me get you some water." Nate left the room and impatiently waited for the glass to fill with water. "Come on, come on." He waited. "Finally!" he said, pulling the glass from the sink, dripping water across the floor as he headed toward the living room. "Here, take a sip and calm down. Tell me what's going on. It can't be anything we can't fix."

"We couldn't fix Ashton."

Nate took a deep breath, instantly holding back a not-so-well-thought-out response that sat on the tip of his tongue, but the urge was a strong one. "What's..." He paused to think just how to say it and chose a simpler response in a calmer voice. *Walk on egg shells.* "Whatever it is with Megan, we can and will fix it. I promise."

"Four teachers just called me, back to back. They're all concerned about her. It's like she turned herself off, Nate, and we didn't even see it. Our own daughter. We're as blind today as we were ten years ago."

"Hey, wait a minute. She'll come around. She's been through hell. We've been through a lot. There were bound to be changes. We'll handle this."

"But..."

"No buts. It's done. When she gets home we'll figure it out and make a plan. Honey, what happened then won't happen now. I promise."

Brandy looked into Nate's eyes and wondered when he had become such a strong man.

Nate looked down at her phone. It was blinking. "Oh, I almost forgot. I let one go to voicemail."

"Well, let's hear it," replied Nate.

Brandy tapped the screen on her phone. "You have one new message... "Hello, Mrs. Renard, this is Sam Babcock, the counselor at Centennial El. We talked a few days ago about socializing Megan. I was wondering if you had a moment to stop in tomorrow. Some things have been brought to my attention that will need immediate correction. Stop in anytime, Brandy. This is important."

Brandy just looked at Nate, her bottom lip quivering. She was about to lose it. Nate sat and held her until she could pull herself together. "Meg should be home in twenty minutes," she said.

Like clockwork, a yellow school bus stopped in front of the house on time. The reflection in a framed picture opposite the window revealed its flashing lights. Megan came be-boppin' up the walk and through the door. She dropped her backpack off at the end of the couch and noticed her mom and dad sitting at the other end.

"Hi, Megan," Brandy greeted.

"How was your day?" asked Nate.

"Fine," she answered and started walking across the living room, sensing that more questions were yet to come.

She didn't quite make it to her room before she was stopped by her mother's voice. "Megan?"

She stopped on a dime and turned. "Yeah, Mom."

"Is there something you want to tell us?"

"Like what?"

"Well, how was school?"

"Fine, school was fine."

"That's not what we are hearing from your teachers, Meg," Nate butted in. Meg said nothing.

"Come here, honey. Let's talk," her mother said. Megan didn't move. She didn't know what this was about, but it didn't sound good. "Megan, please." She pointed to the couch. Megan still didn't move, but she now knew she was probably in trouble.

"Megan! Sit your butt down. Now!" Ordered Nathan. She sat, not saying a word.

"Megan, your math teacher said you've been falling asleep a lot in class. Is this true? Haven't you been sleeping at night?"

Still no response.

"A few other teachers called as well, saying you're not doing the work. Even in gym. No participation. What's going on?"

Still silence.

"Answer your mother, Meg!" Nate said.

Megan started tearing up. "I can't think. I can't concentrate on anything for very long. I haven't been sleeping since he's been gone. I miss Ash." She finally spilled, tears beging to flow.

"Oh, Megan, we're so sorry. We all miss Ash, but life has to go on, honey. You have to do well in school. Do you understand?" asked her mom. Meg nodded her head.

"Is there something you want to talk about, Megan?"

"No, Mom. I'll try harder. I promise," she answered.

"That's my girl," said Nate.

"Thank you, Meg. You know anytime something's bothering you, you can always come to us, right?

"Sure, Mom. Can I go now?"

Brandy and Nate nodded simultaneously. She jumped from the couch and ran to her room, slamming the door behind her.

Brandy got up to go after her, but Nate held her back. "We gave her the opportunity to open up. If we chase her down, she'll just drift farther. Let's see what the counselor has for us tomorrow.

•••

CHAPTER 24

The next morning, Brandy drove Megan to school so she could talk to Sam, the counselor, again.

As always, she knocked before entering.

"Brandy, come in. It's great to see you again. Can I take your jacket?"

Brandy immediately got that uneasy feeling again of being undressed by someone's eyes. "No, I'm fine, thank you." She wrapped the coat snugly around her and tied it tighter. There was something about this man that she didn't like. "What's this all about?" she asked.

"Well, it's rather complicated. Actually, I was just checking Megan's file to see how well the after-school activities were going for her, when I noticed four separate progress reports from four different teachers in her file."

"Oh, I see."

"I flagged Mrs. Tartonnie down in the hallway and

talked to her about her report. She told me that she caught Megan drawing a picture of a crow in her math book during class. Do you know about any of this, Mrs. Renard?"

"Yes, they all called me. I didn't know about the drawing though. She is very artistic."

"The teacher did mention it was quite good, but, Brandy, what I really called you down here for is what her gym teacher told me. He said he hadn't mentioned this to you on the phone. Please, sit down."

Brandy sat, her palms starting to sweat. She was quite nervous and wasn't at all prepared for what she was about to hear. She wished Nate had come with her.

"Mrs. Renard," Sam paused, knowing how sensitive the subject was. "Do you know what 'cutting' means?"

Brandy's eyes couldn't get any bigger. "What?"

"The term 'cutting.'"

"I heard what you said. I don't know what you're talking about, but I don't like the sounds of it."

"Let me get you some water."

"No, I'm fine. Tell me now."

"It's a way that kids, and some adults, for that matter, deal with issues and mental stress. They cut themselves with a razor blade or any sharp object. The physical pain temporarily takes their mind off whatever it is that is currently bothering them."

Brandy, now with her hand covering her mouth, felt ill.

She stood and asked where the closest ladies' room was. The counselor directed her to the one in the main office. She rushed in and vomited in the sink. Afterward, she splashed water on her face and dug into her purse for her phone to call Nate.

"Hello?" Nate answered.

Brandy was in tears. She tried to speak, but no words came out.

"Brandy? Are you there? Is that you? Brandy, talk to me. What's wrong?"

A few minutes had passed, and the counselor was getting worried. He sent a secretary in to check on Brandy and found her passed out on the floor.

"Brandy! Are you there? Brandy, please."

The secretary heard the voice on the phone and picked it up.

"Hello, who is this?" she asked.

"Who is this? Where is my wife?"

"This is the secretary at Centennial Elementary. I just found your wife passed out on the restroom floor. I have to call 911."

"Don't you hang up on me!" The phone switched to dial tone. "Dammit!"

Nate slapped the lid of his laptop down, grabbed his coat, and flew out of his office.

"Nate, is everything all right?" his boss yelled as he saw

him dash past his door, practically taking out the water cooler.

"I'll tell you later!" Nate didn't stop to chat. He yelled down the hall as he left.

Normally, Nathan was a pretty mellow guy on the road. One would never see road rage in his eyes, except for today. He reached his vehicle and floored it, spinning wildly out of the parking lot and onto the street where he made a left turn from the right-hand lane on a yellow light.

Meanwhile, at the school, the secretary called 911, as well as the school nurse, for assistance. Brandy was now conscious, sitting upright on the leather sofa in the restroom. The counselor tried his best to calm her down. The paramedics arrived about two minutes before Nate. They went right to work checking Brandy's vitals. "So far, so good," one of the medics said.

Nate came running through the front door of the school. He didn't bother stopping for the guard, so the guard ran after him. The guard caught up to Nate, who had skidded past the office door. He backtracked right into the guard's arms and was pointed in the right direction. They had been expecting him.

"Honey, are you all right?" he asked, doing his best to get closer.

A couple of the teachers from the crowd that had formed outside the entrance held him back. "Please, sir, give her some room. Stay back."

"I'm her husband."

A paramedic waived him in.

Nate knelt down before her. "Honey, are you all right? What's going on?"

"She fainted, sir," a paramedic interrupted. "She'll be fine."

The counselor looked at Nate. *I don't get it, he* thought to himself. *What is she doing with someone like that?* "Nate?" he said.

"Yes, who are you?" he questioned.

"Sam Babcock, the school counselor. I'll be able to fill you in, if you like, once things settle down."

"That would be great. Thank you. But I would like to hear it from my wife first, if you don't mind."

Brandy shook her head. "Let him explain, hon. I don't think I'll be able to."

"Are you sure?"

Brandy nodded.

"Would you like us to take you in to get checked out, ma'am?" one of the medics asked.

She shook her head, no. "No, thank you. I'll be fine now."

"Very well. I'm not going to argue that. You check out fine here. I just needed to offer." The medic started to pack his gear and move out of the way. "I just need you to sign here."

"What's this?" Nate asked.

"Just a paper saying she refused any further treatment, that's all. Just procedure."

"Are you sure, honey?"

"Yes, I'm fine, Nate. Let's get out of this bathroom and go talk to the counselor together. There are things you need to know."

Nate looked over at the counselor with a concerned look.

"Whenever you two are ready," he offered.

Nate extended an arm to Brandy and helped her from the couch. Stubborn, she refused and got up on her own and led the way back to the guidance office. Feeling a little unstable, she eventually grabbed hold of Nate's arm along the way.

The counselor broke the news to Nate. Nate just stared off into the distance and didn't say a thing. At least not right away. He took time to absorb it all like a sponge before falling apart himself. All he could think about was losing another child.

Brandy consoled him.

Nate finally spoke. "Cutting? What do we do?" He was just as oblivious to the term as Brandy had been. "Kids actually do this? What is wrong with today's kids? I've never heard of this before."

"It's actually been around a long time, Nate. It's just more prevalent now. It's always kind of a hush-hush thing when families first hear of it. People are quite embarrassed by it, but you would be surprised how many do it, and hide it well."

"It's absurd that anyone would actually do that."

"Just think of it this way, Nate. You've cut yourself before, right? Everyone has, by accident, of course. It hurts. Even when we don't expect it, it still hurts. Can you imagine the pain that these kids are going through to want to self-inflict that kind of pain, just so it will override everything else they feel?"

"Have you seen any cuts on her?" Nate asked his wife.

"No, not a one."

"They hide the cuts from view. Usually, clothing will cover the cuts quite well. The stomach area is quite popular, along with the thighs, above the skirts and shorts line."

"I see. So where do we go from here?"

"I'm afraid, because of liability, Nate, I can't tell you what to do. But you have to do something for her, and quickly." Sam handed him a brochure. "There are programs available, depending on the seriousness. Hospitalization is always an option."

"You mean a psych ward?"

"Precisely, but it shouldn't be needed in your case. Now look, I'm saying too much already."

"Well, thank you for what you've done so far. Nate looked at his watch. We have to go so we're home before she gets off the bus." He reached to shake the counselor's hand,

and when he did, the counselor crammed a business card into his hand and whispered, "Off the record, my boy cut for two years."

Nate shook his head and mouthed the words *thank you* before he left. He stuffed the card in his shirt pocket.

It was another quiet ride home until Brandy, out of nowhere, asked, "What did he give you?"

"Excuse me?"

"The counselor gave you something. I saw it. What was it?"

"It was a card. I'm not really sure if it was his card or a card to whoever he's recommending."

"I thought he said he couldn't recommend anything because of liability."

"He did, but he also whispered to me, 'Off the record, my son cut for two years.'"

"Can I see it?"

"Sure." Nate reached in his pocket and pulled out the crumpled business card with the counselor's private cell number on it.

•••

CHAPTER 25

The next day, Megan left for school and forgot her backpack on the floor by the front door. Brandy ran across it while cleaning up the house and was going to take it over to the school, but she decided to take a peek inside first.

Brandy carefully pulled book after book from the bag and started flipping through them as fast as she could. The math book flipped right open to the drawing of a crow in an outside margin of the page. "Wow, it is good," she claimed. She then opened Megan's sketchpad, and before she realized it, minutes turned into hours. She was in awe as she flipped through page after page of beautiful drawings. Among the drawings were poems and short stories that Megan had handwritten as well. She couldn't believe that her little seven-year-old girl was this gifted. Her stories where detailed, and more than a few were more disturbing than she would have liked. Some were about teasing and bullying, one even mentioning the fight on the bus.

The fight was detailed as if Megan were reporting the whole event to the news. Brandy wondered how many of her daughter's stories were true and how many were embellished. Brandy was now concerned. *Are these the red flags that we're suppose to be looking for?*

Not all of the stories were disturbing though. Some were happy, and most had something to do with Ash or the animals that kept him company over the years. Brandy loved the way Megan illustrated the animal stories. They were filled with drawings of squirrels, birds, rabbits, butterflies, and more.

Brandy was about to pack the books away when she ran across specific notes about Ashton with details Megan could not possibly have known on her own. Brandy read a little more before snapping the book shut as soon as she realized what she was looking at. *These are notes for a book she's writing about her brother.* As much as she wanted to keep reading, she knew that she shouldn't. She packed everything back in the bag as best as she remembered, then noticed the time.

"Oh my, she'll be home soon." She placed the backpack by the door where she'd found it and went on with her day.

•••

CHAPTER 26

A loud bell filled the ears of every young child and teacher at Centennial Elementary. School had begun.

"Okay, everyone. Let's settle down now. Today is going to be a writing period. I want all of you to work on your stories the entire hour. Deadline is approaching fast, so please, if you can't find the words to write today, try and test yourself by forcing them out of you. Go ahead and get your notebooks out and begin writing.

The teacher retired to her office at the back of the classroom to catch up on grading a few papers while the students wrote. It wasn't long before the noise level in the classroom grew too loud for her to concentrate, so she got back up to take a look. The noise came to a complete halt the minute she was noticed standing in the doorway of the classroom. She made her rounds, checking to see what each student was up to.

She approached Megan from behind and noticed that

she wasn't writing, nor did she have her notebook on her desk. In fact, the teacher didn't see any book bag at all. "Megan?" she said.

Megan turned in her seat. "Yes, Mrs. Pratt."

"Where is your notebook?"

"Sorry, I accidentally left my backpack at home this morning."

"Oh, I see." The teacher walked by and pulled a fresh notepad from the top drawer of her desk, along with a freshly sharpened pencil. "Here you go, Meg." She handed her a pencil and placed the notepad in front of her.

"But my story is at home," she said.

"The last time I looked, you didn't have a whole lot done on it. Can you start over or maybe start something new?"

"I'll try," Meg said. She grabbed the pencil, and it wasn't long before Megan started writing. She wrote for an hour straight, pausing only to go to the restroom. While she was gone, the teacher came snooping and was shocked to see all the work Meg had done in that short of time.

When Megan returned, she found Mrs. Pratt at her desk. "Excuse me, Mrs. Pratt. Did you read my story?" she asked in front of everyone.

"No, Megan, I just glanced at it to see how you're doing."

"Well, that's good because it isn't finished, and I don't want anyone to read it until it is."

"Oh, well, all right. I'm just so glad you're writing again."

"Me too. The story just came to me all of a sudden. I need to get back to it now."

The teacher backed out of the way and watched Megan write from afar. Megan's little hand flew across the paper. The teacher was in awe. This went on for days. Not only had it happened at school, but it happened at home as well. Megan was so proud of herself that she showed the teacher right away what she had accomplished at home.

"That's great, Megan. Keep up the good work!" And she did. She went right back to her desk and didn't stop writing until the class was over.

Mrs. Pratt couldn't wait to tell Megan's mother. She picked up the phone and dialed her number.

"Hello," she answered.

"Mrs. Renard?"

"Yes."

"This is Mrs. Pratt again, from Centennial El."

Brandy was not enthused about talking to her again.

"What's up, Mrs. Pratt?" Brandy asked with shortened breath.

"I just wanted to let you know that whatever you are doing for Megan, keep it up. What a change. She hasn't stopped writing."

"What?"

"It's true. She hasn't stopped since I gave her a pad of paper and pencil earlier this week."

"Wow, that's great news, Thanks so much for calling."

"Oh, you're very welcome, and thank you. Whatever you did, it's working! Goodbye."

Hmm, that was a weird call, Brandy thought. *We haven't really done anything.*

Brandy was excited to hear what Megan had accomplished. She nervously waited in the living room, pretending to watch TV. In reality, she was watching for the bus.

The bus pulled up and flipped its flashers on. Megan bounced down the steps like she had a renewed spring in her step. She checked the mail at the street, then skipped up the walkway.

"Hi, Meg!" Brandy said as soon as she popped through the door.

"Hi, Mom. What's up?" Meg was all smiles.

"Not much. Did you have a good day?"

"Sure did, Mom. Sorry, no time to chat. I have to go write some things down before I forget. They've been on my mind all the way home."

"Oh, all right. You better not forget."

Megan dashed into her room and closed the door behind her.

Brandy followed not too far behind. "Megan, you know

the rules. The door must stay open all the time, all right?" The latch released and the door swung wide, hitting the adjacent wall. "All right, no problem, Mom."

"Thank you."

A moment later, Nate came through the door.

"Hi, sweetheart. You're home early."

Nate dropped his briefcase to the floor and slid it against the wall with his foot. "Hi, hon," he greeted as he tossed his keys into the wooden bowl centered on the hallway table. "Yeah, not much going on today. How are you?"

Brandy was all smiles. "Great!"

"Where's Megan?"

"Oh, she's in her room, writing."

"Writing? Really?"

"Yeah, her teacher, Mrs. Pratt called and said she's been writing non-stop since Monday."

"Wow, what's gotten into her?"

"She said to keep doing whatever it is we're doing, because it's working."

"Oh, but we really haven't done anything."

"I know," Brandy replied with a quizzical look. She continued, "Whatever it is, I hope it lasts."

"So, what now?"

They both took turns walking past Megan's room, sneaking peeks. Every time, she was at her desk, writing. Brandy even brought her dinner and let her eat in her room just so she could spy over Megan's shoulder.

"Everything okay, honey?"

"Fine, Mom. Thanks."

"Megan, can I ask you a question?"

"Make it quick."

Make it quick? Brandy chuckled after repeating it in her mind. "I was just wondering, why the change. Don't get me wrong, it's good. In fact, it's great, but did something happen?"

"Not sure, Mom. Ever since Mrs. Pratt gave me this pad of paper and pencil, all I want to do is write and sketch again. I'm not sure where the words are coming from. I'm just writing them down as fast as I can."

While holding the pencil up to her mom, Megan noticed something on it. On the top of the pencil near the number 2 was an engraving. It was in the shape of a heart, similar to the heart that Megan had carved on the tree out back. Her eyes got big and bright, and an overwhelming feeling fell over her, while warm thoughts of the past rushed through her. *Ash!* "I have to keep writing, Mom."

"Well, okay. Don't let me get in your way." Brandy stepped back and watched for a second from the doorway before disappearing around the corner.

The next day, Megan asked her teacher if she could have another pencil. The one she was using was getting short and hard to handle from use.

"Sure, Meg, here you go." The teacher handed her a

pencil from her top drawer.

"Thank you, Mrs. Pratt." Meg looked at the pencil and twirled it around in her fingers, but something was wrong. You could see it in her eyes. She tugged on Mrs. Pratt's sleeve to gain her attention.

"Yes, Megan? Did you need something else?"

"Can I have a different one?" Meg asked, holding the pencil near her face. "Please?"

"Sure, is there something wrong with that one?" she asked while digging in her top drawer again.

"I want the same kind you gave me the other day," Meg meekly requested, showing her the small stub that was left of the pencil.

"A pencil is a pencil, Meg. They are both standard number-two pencils."

"But…" Meg had to think of something fast. "I want it all to look the same." She went on and on about how she liked the other pencil. "This one has a heart carved into it."

"Let me see. By golly, you're right. Let me dig some more." Mrs. Pratt dug deeper into her drawer, and, sure enough, she had one more. She handed the pencil to Megan, who was now all smiles.

"Here we go," Mrs. Pratt said when she held up a brand new, unsharpened pencil. She sharpened the tip and handed it to Megan. "This looks to be my last one, Megan."

Megan smiled and asked, "Well, where did you get them?"

"Wow. You're full of questions today."

"I just really like these pencils."

"Well, I think I bought them at Walgreen's down the road, if you must know, but they were on clearance. I doubt there are any left. You have that one, though. Now go create something special with it."

Megan thanked her for the pencil and skipped back to her desk. She wrote and drew pictures from then on, also at home, right up until the time she went to bed.

Saturday morning, the sun shone brightly. If Ash were still there, Megan would have been out back playing under the tree. But since he was gone, Megan found a new place to hide out: her desk. There she was, writing away. Nate and Brandy eavesdropped a few times to see what she was writing. Each time, Megan quickly covered up her work so they couldn't see. "Not until it's finished," was her typical response before shooing her folks away.

Her parents left the room and stopped in the hallway. "I'm just going to ask her," Brandy told Nate.

"Just let her be. We'll know in good time."

"Is that what you're afraid of? You're looking for signs, aren't you?"

"Isn't that what we're suppose to do, Nate? You know, find them before something happens again."

"Well, yeah, but she has a right to her space too, doesn't she?"

"Better safe than sorry, Nate."

"Yeah, you're right. So what are you going to do, rip it out of her hands?"

"No, of course not. I'm just going to ask and see what she says," Brandy said while walking back into Meg's room. Nate followed.

"Megan?"

"Yes, Mom."

"I'm sorry, it's killing me. I have to know. What are you writing?"

"It's a surprise, Mom."

"A surprise? For who?"

"You and Dad, but if you must know, this story is about my brother, Ash. Kind of his life story."

Nate gave Brandy an odd look.

"But you weren't around when he was alive. How?"

"Somehow the words are there, Mom. I can't explain it."

"Do you need help?"

"Maybe. So far I don't, though, but maybe if I get stuck. I'll let you know."

Brandy smirked at Nate.

"Just know that we're here if you need us, all right?"

"You bet, Mom. Thanks."

The two of them walked into the kitchen, leaving

Megan to her writing. "I haven't seen her this happy in a long time."

"Yeah, it's great, though I don't see how or why."

"Me neither."

Two hours went by. Nate and Brandy were sitting at the kitchen table, enjoying a cup of coffee over idle conversation.

"The backyard just doesn't look the same," mentioned Nate.

"It's sad, but we're getting through it. How about getting a plaque made for Ashton and fastening it to the stump somehow," Brandy suggested.

"That's a wonderful idea, dear."

They finished their coffee and peeked in at Megan one more time to see what she felt like eating for dinner. They walked into her room.

"Shh," Brandy whispered back to Nate, with her finger in front of her mouth. "I think she's fallen asleep."

Nate took a look over her shoulder. Megan was slumped over her desk, her head resting on her arm. "She's not asleep," Nate said when he saw her move. They looked over her shoulder and saw their little girl struggling to hold onto a tiny pencil. She had worn another pencil down to a nub.

Nathan ran to his home office and grabbed two new pencils from his desk and laid them on Megan's desk next to her. "Careful, they're sharp."

Megan stopped, grabbed one, and thanked him with a smile before continuing her writing, before she lost her train of thought.

"Anything special you want for dinner, Meg?" Brandy asked.

"Mac 'n' cheese, Mom, with hotdogs," she answered. Mac 'n' cheese was one of her favorite meals.

"You got it! Macaroni and cheese, coming right up," Brandy replied.

"Don't forget the hotdogs," she said over her shoulder.

Brandy nodded, and they left for the kitchen. A few minutes later, Brandy returned with Megan's dinner. When she did, she noticed Megan struggling once again with the nubby pencil.

"Megan, why aren't you using the pencils your dad gave you?"

"They don't work, Mom."

"They don't work?"

"I can't write with them."

"Well, why not? Are they too big?"

"They're just not the same."

Brandy set the macaroni and cheese down and looked at the pencils. "Standard number-two pencils. They're the same, dear."

"No, they're not, Mommy. They're not the same at all."

"What do you mean, honey? Don't they write?" Brandy

scribbled on the edge of one of her pages. Megan instantly started yelling and crying.

"No! No! Stop," she cried out, just before jumping onto her bed, bawling her eyes out. She buried her face in her pillow and kicked her feet in a tantrum.

"Meg, stop it right now," Brandy ordered.

Nate came running into the room. "What's going on?"

"She doesn't like the pencils you gave her."

"What? All of this is over pencils? What's wrong with the pencils, Meg?" He grabbed one from Brandy's hand and looked down at it. He rolled it between his fingers. "Looks all right to me," he shrugged.

"She said they're not the same," Brandy replied, raising her voice over Megan's whimpers. "Megan, that's enough. Now get up here and tell your dad what is wrong with these pencils."

"No, they're not the same!" she yelled back and continued to cry, punching at her pillow.

"Wow, she hasn't acted like this in years," Brandy said.

"There must be something to it." Nate sat at the edge of the bed. "Megan. Megan, honey, calm down and talk to daddy." Nate was always the calm one in the family.

Brandy handled things a little differently, usually in a much louder tone. "Come on, Megan. Help Daddy figure this out for you."

Still nothing.

"Show me what the difference is, honey, and we'll get you new ones," said Nate.

That's what she wanted to hear. She stopped crying and rolled over to the side of the bed in an instant.

"Okay, so what's the difference, honey?"

Nate took one of the new pencils and wrote his name on a scrap of paper. "Works fine for me. Here, honey, you try." He handed Meg the pencil.

She refused.

Brandy ripped the pencil from Nate's hand and stuck it in Megan's. "Show us!"

Meg gripped the pencil and placed the lead to paper. She was still as a statue. "See?" she said, almost in tears.

"Well, write something. Go ahead," her mom prodded.

She tried again. Nothing. "I don't know what to write, Mom."

"Write your name, sweetheart. Like we did," suggested Nate.

"That's only a name, Dad. That's not very meaningful."

"Are you saying you can only write meaningful things with these?" Nate opened his hand, exposing the two pencil nubs. "What's the difference?"

Megan rolled one of the nubby pencils and pointed to what was left of an engraved heart.

Nate looked confused. There wasn't enough left to tell what the engraving had been. She then pointed to the other nub, slightly longer than the first.

As soon as Nate saw it, visions of the heart that Megan carved in the tree came to mind. They were identical. "It's the heart," he said.

"Heart?" questioned Brandy.

"Yes, the heart that Meg carved on the tree. It's right here." He pointed. Brandy couldn't believe it.

"Wow, what a coincidence," she added.

Nate wasn't so convinced it was a coincidence. In fact, he was sure that it wasn't.

Nate looked closer at the pencil. Most of the name had been shaved away from sharpening. There was a number two at the top, just above the heart, but the manufacturer's name below it was mostly gone. One of the pencil nubs had the letter G and what looked like part of an E or a B. GB made no sense, so Nate assumed it was GE or something.

"Where did you get these, Megan?" asked Nate. "We'll go get some more," Nate said, assuming it would be easy.

"From my teacher, Mrs. Pratt." she answered.

"Does she have anymore?"

Megan shook her head, no. "She gave me the last one. She said she got them down the road, but they probably didn't have anymore."

"Where down the road?"

"Wall… something."

"Walmart?"

"Yeah, I think."

"We'll check." This put a smile on Megan's face. "In the meantime, can you try to use the new pencils I gave you?"

Megan nodded with a weak smile.

Later that day, Nate was out and about and pulled into Walmart's parking lot. He picked up a few things for dinner, then headed over to the school and office supplies. He searched up and down the aisles countless times, but no luck. He didn't find any pencils with hearts engraved on them, but he did find some pencils that had "GENERAL" stamped on them. *That's it!* he thought to himself. *I'll just call the manufacturer.*

Nate purchased a pack of number-two GENERAL pencils, hoping to research the company later when he got home.

Nate's heart melted when he saw his two favorite girls anxiously waiting at the door.

"I'm so sorry, I didn't find any." He paused as he watched their facial expressions go south. "But I think I found who made them." He turned to Megan. "Will you get me the two nubby pencils?" Megan quickly ran to her room and returned with them in her hand. Nate lined the longest pencil nub up with the ones in the package. Sure enough, it was a match.

"Yes!" he said aloud. "I'll contact them tomorrow. We'll find them, honey. Don't you worry."

•••

CHAPTER 27

"Hi Nathan, whatcha doing?" Brandy asked as she entered his home office. Nate sat at his desk in front of the computer with his palm supporting his head.

"Oh hi, dear. Come in and have a seat. I want to run something by you."

"Uh oh, that doesn't sound good. What gives?"

"I've been giving it a lot of thought. In fact, it's been looming in the back of my mind since the day they took Ash. I just want an outside opinion on this, that's all. I may be reading way too much into it."

"Ok, shoot."

"Well, remember when Megan brought us the leaf and we rushed downtown to show my boss?"

"Well, of course I do. It was one of the best and worst days of my life."

"Yeah, mine too. Anyway, I've been doing some

figuring and…" He paused, trying to regain his train of thought. "Well, don't you think it's kind of strange that they would take the tree on that very same day? The very same two-and-a-half-hour window?"

"I guess. I never really thought about it, Nate. What are you getting at?"

"I've made a few calls to some tree trimmers. I told them what we had and asked about how long it would take to take down a tree of that size and get it out of here without a trace. You know what he said?" Brandy shook her head. "Well, I'll tell you what he *didn't* say. He didn't say three hours, and he didn't say four. What he did tell me is, with the right equipment, he could probably have a crew there, take down the tree, and haul it away in less then 2 hours, if he had to. He also said not to tell any of his customers that. It would put him out of business."

"Okay… Go on," she chuckled.

"We were gone for approximately two and a half, maybe three, hours. Meaning, if we would have stayed home an extra fifteen minutes or gotten home twenty minutes earlier, there would have been a good chance of seeing them."

"Coincidence?"

"Maybe, but the more I think about it, the more I think not."

"So what do you really think?"

"I'm not for sure, but my gut is telling me that they had to know we were going to be gone and for how long."

"Makes sense."

"And the only person who knew that was Stan. I don't want to think that he had something to do with it, but things add up and point in his direction."

"What, you think he called someone to take care of this while he was taking care of us?"

"I don't know, maybe. All I'm saying is, he had the time and the motive. He's been taking a lot of flak over this, and, well, it's an election year. I just know I felt all along that we were being stalled over there."

"Funny you should say that. I felt the same way, sitting in the restaurant. Especially when he was so eager to have the judge sign the papers, even on a Saturday. He probably just left to see if the tree was down or not so we could go freely. So, what now?"

"I don't know. Nothing, I guess. I don't have any proof. It was just bothering me, and I needed to talk it out. That's all. Thanks."

"Anytime, but now you've made me curious."

"Someday we will know the truth. It just won't be today. Somebody is bound to talk sometime."

•••

CHAPTER 28

"Hi Boss..." Nate stopped mid-thought as he rounded the corner to his office. His boss was busy talking on the phone.

"Yeah, Gabe, listen, I hate to cut you off short, but I have to run... Yeah, okay, we'll talk later, okay? Yeah, I'll call you." Stan hung up the phone. "Hey, Nate, come on in. What's up?"

"Oh, nothing really, boss. Sorry, I didn't mean to interrupt. Sounded important. I don't think I ever properly thanked you for everything you did to try and help us."

"Oh, that's all right, Nate. Considering what had happened, that's completely understandable."

"Well, I wanted to thank you anyway. You didn't have to do what you did, you know?"

Stan looked at him funny, like maybe he misunderstood what Nate was trying to say. He shook it off. "I was just trying to help, Nate."

"Yeah, I know." Nate turned to walk out of Stan's office but paused briefly at the door. "Oh, I almost forgot. I'm going to do whatever it takes to find the bastards who did it. I won't rest until I do, so if you hear anything, I sure would appreciate a call."

Stan swallowed hard. "I'll be all ears, Nate."

"Thanks, Stan."

Nate walked down the hall, wondering why Stan had gotten off the phone as soon as he had walked in. He tried to piece together the words from the other side of the conversation. He could make the right words fit easily enough, but it was just speculation. *Stan sure acted nervous enough*, Nate thought. But Nate hadn't seen enough to totally convince him that Stan was involved, even though his gut feeling said Stan was guilty as hell. He would have to do more digging.

That evening after work, Nate saw Stan leave the city office and decided to follow him awhile. Stan didn't turn in his usual direction to go home. Instead, he traveled north and pulled into a bar just down the road. Nate drove past, then came back a few minutes later, and drove around the parking lot. There it was, just what he was looking for: Stan's car, parked on the other side of a pickup truck, hidden from view. The pickup was lettered, "Gabe's Tree Service."

Stan had talked about Gabe, his fishing buddy, all the

time at the office but never mentioned him owning a tree service. Not even when Nate had asked Stan if he new anyone who knew trees, when they were trying to identify the tree in the backyard.

Strange, Nate thought. *Very strange.*

Nate sat in the parking lot for a while, thinking. As much as he wanted to, he couldn't think of any reason to go inside. He didn't drink, and it would look too suspicious if he were seen. He took a photo with his phone of the two parked vehicles and left, unaware that his boss was watching through the window of the bar.

Hmmmm, was that Nate? Stan thought nervously.

Nate didn't drive anything unique. There were millions of cars like his on the road every day. The same make and color were popular, but Stan had an uneasy feeling about this one. He shook his head and continued his business by handing Gabe, sitting across from him, a thick envelope of cash.

"Hi, hon, I'm home," Nate yelled as he walked through the door.

"Hi, Nate, pizza's on the counter."

"I confronted Stan today. Well, maybe 'confronted' isn't the best word to use. We talked."

"Oh?"

"He seemed nervous. I caught him in the middle of a phone call that obviously wasn't intended for my ears, so he cut it short."

"Really?"

"Yeah, I didn't think much of it at the time. It was just Gabe, his fishing buddy. It was weird, though. I didn't find out why it was so weird until I followed him after work to a bar down the street. You know the one, the Road House."

"That dive? It sure has gone downhill."

"Yeah, a good place to meet up with shady people, I guess."

"Hey, we met there."

Nate chuckled and took a bite of pizza. "He met Gabe there."

"His old fishing partner, right?"

"So he says. He failed to let us know that Gabe is also a tree expert. He parked next to Gabe's truck, which advertised tree trimming. You would think he'd know a little about trees."

"I thought Stan said he didn't know anyone who knew anything about trees."

"I was about to check that out online." Nate sat at the computer and hit the power button to boot it up. "Come on, this thing takes forever to boot anymore."

"Yeah, we should take it in to get it cleaned up."

"Let's do that. I'll drop it off at Tim's later today."

Tim was well known in the area for computer repair. He worked out of his house and had pretty low rates.

After another slice of pizza, the computer's user screen finally came up. Nate hit his name and then launched Internet Explorer. He began to type, but not very well. "Googel.com. Um, goo gel.com. Shit. Oogle.com" This one worked, but took him to a porn site. "Oh my." He fat-fingered his way through several different spellings before finally taking time to tap out the right keys. "There. Wow." Finally the right page appeared, although the previous one looked a hell of lot more interesting.

"Geeze, Nate, do you want me to drive?" Brandy chuckled.

"I got this." He slowly pecked out, "Gabe tree service" in the search line and clicked the "Search" button.

The screen read, "Did you mean Gabe's Tree Service?"

"Grr, yes!" He clicked the underlined words. Hundreds of references appeared on the screen.

"Type in the area," offered Brandy.

Nate did, which narrowed the search down to just one. Nate clicked on the link. Sure enough, it was Gabe, the same guy. The front page showed a photo of his truck, the same truck that Stan parked next to at the bar.

"I've been to this site before, when I was looking for tree doctors. It just looked like a tree-trimming service, so I clicked away. Sorry, I…"

"That's all right, dear. We're here now."

They continued to click through page after page filled with job sites, descriptions, and service information. They clicked on the "Service" tab and saw nothing about being a tree doctor, so Brandy was right—he was just a tree trimmer, but a tree trimmer still should know their trees.

The "Info" tab was next. Recent jobs. They scanned through photo after photo, some showing before-and-after shots. Some workers even posed in front of their largest take, as if they were big game hunters proud of their kill. Then...

"Nate, look." Brandy pointed to the screen. Tears filled her eyes. "Isn't that our..."

"Bingo!" Nate interrupted, throwing his arm around Brandy's waist. He pulled her close, seeing that she was upset. "That's our tree, right there! Damn them! I knew it. I knew Stan had something to do with it. He kept us at his office, waiting for Gabe, his fishing buddy, to finish the job." Nate was furious.

"But, Nate, wait. You're probably right, but this doesn't prove anything."

"Yeah, yeah, you're right, but we're getting closer. How do I save this?"

"Well, you can bookmark the page, but he could take the photos down anytime, Nate. You should do screen shots so we'll have proof that they were on the site."

"Screen shots? Here, you do it." Nate got up from the seat feeling defeated. "You take the helm."

Brandy sat down and started saving screen shot after screen shot to a folder on the desktop. After about the tenth one, she decided to look for a better way. She searched online and found an app to download the entire site.

"You're a genius."

"That's why you love me."

Nate reached around her from behind and planted a kiss on the back of her neck while his hands slithered around her arms to catch a feel of her breasts. He squeezed. "Yeah, that's one of the reasons," he whispered into her ear. She slapped Nate's hands away. "Nathan, not now. What's this link to?" The link simply read "USES." She clicked on it. It listed all of the things that Gabe's Tree Service did with the trees once they have loaded them up and hauled them away. Firewood, of course, was first on the list, with huge savings for the consumer. They didn't have to haul the wood away at all. They would just neatly stack it in the customer's yard. Next of the list was hauling the wood to a sawmill. "Sawmill" was a hyperlink, which took them to a page listing local sawmills. Next on the "USES" list was selling the wood to artisans who use the raw wood for arts and crafts, making natural tables and chairs for a rustic cabin look. Next was a link that read, "Specialty."

Brandy didn't hesitate. She clicked and there it was, a pencil factory that bought raw wood from tree trimmers. They listed the types of trees they accepted, cedar being the top-dollar payout. But they also accepted some maple, oak, and birch, among others. At the bottom, printed in red with an asterisk, was, *NO ASH TREES ACCEPTED!"

"They knew, and they still chopped it down!" But in all

honesty, they probably hadn't known until afterward. Once the tree was down, one of the crew probably recognized a leaf as a box elder, but they couldn't stop midway. They had to get rid of the evidence, so they took it there. Nate pointed to the picture of the pencil factory.

Nate clicked on the photo. It enlarged on the screen. It was old and blurry, but not so blurry that he couldn't make out what the sign said. "General Pencil Factory." This was the same place Nate had sent an email to earlier that morning.

•••

CHAPTER 29

After lunch, Nate disconnected the computer and placed it in the car. He had a few errands to run, one of which was to drive past Gabe's Tree Service to have a look around. He wanted to get a feel for the place and see what type of business it really was.

The first stop, though, was to drop the computer off to Tim for repair.

"Hey, Tim, what's up, man?" Nate said as he walked through the service door to Tim's garage.

"Nate, how are you? Man, it's been a long time. How's the city been treating you?"

"Same old, same old, Tim, but it's a job."

"Yeah, one with a pension. That's great. What can I do for you? I just got done working on your boss's machine."

A light bulb went off in Nate's head. "Oh? Home or office?"

"Home. Hey, you should earn some brownie points and take it with you. It will save him a trip to pick it up."

"Sure," Nate said, thinking it couldn't get any better than that. "I'd be happy to. As for mine, it's just running super slow, Tim. It takes forever to do anything."

Tim looked up Nate's account. "Well, it's been a while, Nate. Almost a year."

"Wow, it's been that long?"

"Sure has. Let me write you up." Tim mumbled a few words as he scanned through the questions on his forms. Password, Nate?"

No response.

"Nate? Earth to Nate. Come in, over."

"I'm sorry, what?" Nate finally replied. He had been deep in thought, coming up with a plan.

"Password?" Tim asked again.

"No, no password." *Damn, I bet Stan has his password-protected.* He drifted off again, blowing his idea out of the water. *Now what?*

"Alrighty, we're all set." Tim ripped off a tag and taped it to the computer and gave Nate the other half.

"Thanks, Tim. How long do you think? We're kind of in a hurry."

"Oh, um, I'm kind of backed up, Nate. We're looking at three to five business days. I could expedite it to the front of the line for an additional $25, if you like. If not, I have to keep it in the order I received it."

"Do it, will ya?"

"Will do, Nate." Tim lifted the computer from the table and carried it to the workbench, then hooked it up to a monitor. He looked at his watch. I should have it for you by the end of the day. I'll call you when it's ready."

"Perfect! Thanks, Tim."

Nate turned to leave but stopped and asked another question. "Oh, Tim. I almost forgot. My daughter, well you know she's at that age when you have to watch everything carefully."

"Yeah, I know exactly what you mean, Nate. What's up, need a key logger on her computer?"

"Key logger? Oh no, I hope I don't need to go that far. I just need access to it. She locked it down with a password. Anything I can do? I would just like to check it out every once in a while, you know."

"I have a daughter myself, Nate. Hang on."

"Oh, how old?"

"She's eight."

"Seven here."

"I'll be right back." Tim left to go to the back room. He returned with a thumb drive. "Here you go. Just put this in, run the program, and with a couple of clicks you're golden."

"That's it?"

"That's it."

"Thanks a million. I'll bring this back when I pick mine up. If I can get the computer away from her, that is."

"Don't worry about it. And besides, you're going to need that every time she puts the password back on. Keep it. I'll just charge it to your bill."

"Great! Thanks." Nate turned to leave again when Tim stopped him.

"Nate?" Nate nervously stopped in his tracks and slowly turned around. "Here, take a copy of Stan's order form with you, so he'll know what he owes." He handed him a copy.

"Oh, thanks." Nate left with Stan's personal computer tucked under his arm. Nate got into his car, feeling uncomfortable about taking Stan's computer home. He was even more nervous about what he was thinking about doing with it. He glanced over at the order form. The line was left blank where it asked for the password. *Great,* he thought, relieved that there was no password. In his burst of excitement, he rounded a corner a little too fast and took it wide. His tires left the pavement, waking him up to reality. *Concentrate!* He would drive past Gabe's place another day. Now his mind was on other things.

Nate got home with Stan's computer, contemplating whether to actually go through with his plan. One deep breath later, he was in the house with it and almost done booting it up. Just in case he needed to copy any files from the computer, Nate plugged his own small, black memory stick into a USB drive on the back of Stan's computer.

"Shit!" Nate said as the computer booted, asking for a password anyway. *Maybe I missed it,* he thought as he ran to get the invoice sitting in the front seat of the car. He didn't get down the front porch steps before he came face to face with Brandy, coming up the walk.

"Hey, Nate, what's your hurry?"

"Hold on. I'll explain in a minute," he said as he jogged past to his car, fumbling with the keys. The keys dropped to the ground. As he bent over to pick them up, he heard someone pull up in his driveway behind him. He looked past his knees and watched the car get closer and closer. Bile quickly filled his throat when he noticed who it was. "Oh, my gosh."

Nate started to panic. He quickly snatched the keys from the ground, unlocked the door, and grabbed the paperwork from the car. Nate took two deep breaths as the car rolled to a stop. He walked up to it. "Hey boss, what's up?" Nate greeted.

"Hi Nate. Listen, I just stopped by Tim's place to check on my computer, and he said you have it."

"Yeah, he talked me into taking it to save you a trip. Guess that didn't work out, did it? Listen, I just took it inside. I didn't want to leave it in the car overnight. I'll grab it. Be right back."

"Thanks, Nate. I appreciate that."

Nate held a finger up, signaling his boss to wait one moment, and ran up to the porch and into the office. Brandy was there admiring the new computer. "Not ours," said Nate as he reached around her to hold the button down to shut it down.

"That's not the proper way to shut..."

"I know, no time," interrupted Nathan. He pulled the cords and carried it out to Stan. He set it in the front seat of the car. "There you go. And, oh, here's the bill he sent with me too."

"Great, thanks a lot, Nate. What's yours in for?"

"My what?"

"Your computer."

"Oh, just a tune-up. It's running really slow. Sorry you had to drive out of your way to pick this up. It was supposed to save you a trip, not cost you more time."

"That's all right. Got it now. Thanks again."

"Anytime, boss."

Nate walked up to the house with his heart beating out of his chest. He crashed on the couch in the living room and didn't say a word until Brandy came looking for him.

Stan didn't get very far down the road when he picked up the bill for his computer. He was curious at the price and what work had been done. He laid his arm on the top of the computer as an armrest. "Damn, that's hot. Hmm." He pulled his arm away. His wrist lay across the power supply. "Shit!" he yelled. "He's been into my computer. Dammit all!"

Stan started to shake uncontrollably. Then sweat ran

down his forehead, stinging his eyes. He grabbed some napkins above the visor and wiped himself down, but it kept coming.

"You want to tell me what the hell that was all about?" Brandy asked, startling Nate with his back turned.

"Shit, you scared me." Nate's nerves were a bit on edge.

"You weren't going to snoop through Stan's computer, were you?"

Nathan cringed like a beaten dog after dumping the wastebasket and spreading it throughout the house. "What did it look like?" he finally asked, rather sarcastically.

"Tell me you weren't going to snoop through Stan's computer!"

"I would, but it would be a lie."

"How did you get it?"

"Tim had it. He asked me to take it with me to save Stan a trip. The temptation was too great for me, I guess."

"I'm so glad he stopped and got it first. You could be in big trouble, doing what you were going to do."

"I know." Shame fell upon Nate's face and certainly didn't help his ego. "Sorry, hon. I'm just trying to find answers, that's all. I need some proof!"

"You need your head examined. You're going to end up in jail!"

Nate's phone rang.

"Hello?"

"Nate? Tim. Hey man, I'm running into some issues with your machine here. A couple of viruses are really giving me hell. It's not going to be ready today like I thought. Tomorrow for sure, bro!"

"That's fine, Tim. No problem. I'll swing by after work

tomorrow."

"Great, thanks Nate. It's my wife's birthday and well, you know, birthday stuff tonight or I would work over to get it done for you."

"Understandable. No problem at all, Tim. We have a laptop here that will get us by for the night if need be. Happy birthday to your wife."

"Thanks, I'll tell her. See you tomorrow."

Nate hung up the phone and looked at his wife. "We still have that laptop, right?"

"Sure, I haven't used it in years though. I hope it boots." She pulled it out of the closet and plugged it in to charge the battery. Nothing happened after hitting the power button.

"Shit."

•••

CHAPTER 30

The next morning, Nate headed straight over to Gabe's Tree Service. It wasn't too far from the park he had grown to know and love. He slowed the car and took photos out the window with his cell phone. He saw nothing really suspicious until he noticed a city truck parked around back—one of the same trucks used by the city to cut down all the ash trees around town. "Hmm, how convenient," Nate said to himself as he snapped a couple more shots. "They sure do have a way of keeping the money in the family. I bet Gabe isn't a friend at all, but a family member." *More research to do tonight*, he thought to himself.

Just then, Gabe backed out of the driveway with the city truck, on his way to a job site to chop down yet another tree. Nate followed for a while, then backed off before turning down Tim's street to pick up his computer.

Nate set the computer up as soon as he walked through

the door. He was quite anxious to find out all he could on Gabe. He recruited Brandy to do the driving. He knew what he wanted, but Brandy's knowledge of the computer and Internet beat Nate's experience by a long shot.

The computer booted. "Wow, that was fast. Look at that." Nate was excited.

"All right, where do we start?" asked Brandy.

"I don't know. Where do you go to find people, and things about them?"

Brandy started with Google. She typed in Gabe's full name and state. The results were endless. She replaced the state with the zip code, which narrowed the search down a lot.

Nate was distracted by something out the window. "Honey, keep looking. I'll be right back." He bolted out the door and dashed across the lawn to his neighbor's house. He pounded on the door. No one answered. A feeling of deja-vu came over him. "Hernandez, I know you're in there, Jim. I say you fess up, dammit! I know you had something to do with this! Open the damn door, you frickin' coward!" He yelled and kicked at the door. Nate left the front door and made his way around the house. He looked in the windows and checked the side doors. He knocked on them all and yelled out Jim's name again. He saw movement inside, but no one came to the door. Minutes later, while working his way to the front of the house again, he was stopped. "Hold it right there. Put your hands on your head and get down on your knees."

"Aw, you've got to be kidding me. Jim, you called the cops on me, man?"

"We're not going to ask you again."

Nate raised his hands out in front of him, shaking them back and forth. "I'm the neighbor. Those guns are not necessary."

"On the ground, now!" an officer barked, but Nate didn't move fast enough. Nate heard a loud blast, and the next thing he knew, he was lying on the ground in convulsions. Every muscle in his body stiffened uncontrollably. The blast was not from a gun but from a Taser. Nate's body was jerking like a fish out of water from the jolt of fifty thousand volts. He was tossed into the back of the squad car, headed for the station.

Brandy jumped in her seat when she heard the blast. Thinking nothing of it, she kept searching for information on Gabe. She clicked on Spokeo.com. She typed in his name and selected the state. Then she selected the town. That narrowed the search drastically. There was only one, and the map matched his address. "This was way too easy," she said. She clicked to find out his spouse's name and instantly found the catch. The website required a membership. *Small price to pay for all that information,* she thought, and didn't hesitate to fill in the pertinent information.

While waiting for the credit card to process, she realized that Nate had been gone for quite a while. She looked around and caught the tail end of a police car driving by, hot, but with no siren. Then she remembered hearing the blast. "Nate!"

An uneasy feeling came over her. She ran to the neighbors' house to check on Nate.

She knocked softly. Jim answered, thinking the cops came back for something. "Oh, hello, Brandy. If you're going to cause a scene too, I will call the cops on you as well."

"What are talking about?"

"Your maniac husband. The police had to Taser him to bring him under control. They hauled him away."

"Taser? What?" She ran back home just as the school bus pulled up.

"He was out of control, Brandy. I had no choice!" yelled Jim as she ran toward home.

•••

CHAPTER 31

"What were you thinking, Nate?" Brandy asked as she drove him home from the police station.

"How was I supposed to know he was going to call the cops?"

"What did you expect? You ran over there like a madman."

Nate rubbed his chest and arms. "Man, I ache." Every muscle he had ached from the Taser.

"You're lucky he didn't press charges."

"Charges for what? I didn't do anything," Nate rebutted.

"Yeah, well you're still lucky." Brandy pulled into the drive. "I'll get dinner on."

"Thanks, dear. I'm going to relax my muscles for a bit."

Nate laid on the couch and closed his eyes. He opened them when he felt someone sit on the opposite end. It was

Megan. Nate sat up.

"Whatcha drawing, little girl? Can I see?" Megan turned her sketchbook away, out of her dad's view. "Aw, come on, please?" She finally gave in and tilted the drawing his way, but she still wouldn't let him hold it. "Wow, that's awesome! Great job!"

The drawing depicted a squirrel sitting on the deck rail in front of the tree, with Ash looking back at the squirrel. Ash always loved the animals.

"Do you have any more?"

The sketchbook was full of drawings, far better than any seven-year-old should have been able to draw. All of the drawings represented the tree in one way or another—birds on the branches, squirrels climbing down the trunk, butterflies fluttering nearby, ants walking up and down the bark like cars on the expressway. Nathan flipped a few more pages, and he came across a close-up drawing of Ash with a heart drawn next to his face, as if someone had carved it.

"This is the heart you carved in the tree, isn't it?"

Megan nodded sadly.

"These are great, Megan. Have you shown these to anyone else? I bet your mother would love to see these, especially the one with the nuthatch walking down the trunk of the tree. That's her favorite bird, you know." Little did they know that her mother had already seen them all.

Megan shook her head, no. She hadn't let anyone see her drawings. Not until today. She just did them for herself, for the pure enjoyment of doing them, just like some of her stories that she had written next to them.

"I have an idea. Let's play a game," suggested Nate. And that's what they did.

Brandy walked down the hall after hearing laughter coming from the other room. She walked a few steps toward the living room and found Nate spending quality time with Megan. She was drawing pictures, and Nate was guessing what they were. It was kind of like Pictionary®, but without the playing cards, and no one was keeping score.

Brandy just stood there, leaning against the doorway. She enjoyed every moment of what she was seeing. It was truly a sight that she lived for.

She looked high up on the bookshelf and grabbed Ashton's photo and placed it on a lower shelf among the others. She certainly didn't need to hide him from Megan anymore. She mouthed the words, "I love you," to the photo, brushed off some dust, then continued to watch the two play.

Megan kept on sketching pictures, this one of a dog. Nate guessed it right away, even the breed. She was good. Brandy was amazed at how Megan took after her brother. Both of them could draw really well.

Then Megan drew a computer and turned it around so Nate could see. He guessed a paper shredder at first. Megan added more details, then a monitor. She turned it around again and, of course, Nate now guessed "toaster." He was just playing games with her now. Megan shook her head and drew a keyboard. "Computer!" he yelled.

Megan, all excited, drew a picture of a thumb. She turned it around.

"Thumbnail?" Nate questioned. Megan shook her head no.

Nate's smile instantly disappeared from his face as his heart sunk deep in his chest.

Brandy noticed the change from afar. "Nate, are you all right?" His face looked flush and his body slowly slumped to the floor.

"Nate!" Brandy yelled and ran to his side. She wrapped her arms around him, holding him up. "What's wrong? Nate, speak to me!"

Nate's face began to lose color, turning pale white. He wasn't breathing right, and his skin turned cold. He began to shake. "Are you having a heart attack?" Brandy asked.

Nate shook his head, no.

"Then what? What is it, Nate?" Brandy started to panic.

"I left my thumb drive plugged into Stan's computer," he finally said in a monotone voice.

Brandy gasped, covering her mouth with her hand. "Oh my gosh." Silence filled the room. Megan continued to draw, oblivious to what was going on.

"What are you going to do?"

"I don't know. Look for another job, I guess."

"Don't be silly. You just have to get it back."

"That's probably easier said than done."

"What's on the drive?"

"To be honest, I don't even know. Probably not much. I was going to copy his files off onto it. I just hope it doesn't have anything personal on it that can lead back to me. That's all the proof he would need to know that I was in his computer, even though I never got that far."

"What thumb drive was it, Nate? Do you remember?"

"It was just a small eight-gig stick, black. I liked it because it had such a small footprint. It was so tiny, you hardly knew it was there."

"Well, let's hope it's hard for Stan to find too."

The next morning, Nate got ready for work as he usually did. He felt a little sick to his stomach and didn't really want to go in, but since his boss never called, he assumed that Stan hadn't found the memory stick yet, or there wasn't any incriminating files on it, which he doubted. He was never that lucky. He had a cup of coffee with a side of Rolaids for breakfast and headed out the door. So far, he hadn't a clue what to do yet.

"Good morning, Nate," Stan said as Nate passed his office door. His door was usually left open, but there was no open-door policy in place. Secrets were all too common in the office.

Nate jumped. Stan never came in so early and hadn't expected him to be there.

"Stan, good morning," Nate stammered, nerves shot. Nate immediately wondered what was up. "Wow, you're up early. What's the occasion?" he asked.

"Have to leave early today, Nate. Wife's having outpatient surgery and I have to take her in.

"Oh, is she all right?"

"They found a spot in her mammogram last week. She's going in for a biopsy; third time in five years. Never amounts to anything, but you never know."

"Well, good luck. I hope it all works out."

"Thanks, Nate." He paused. "Are you all right? You're not looking well."

Nate hesitated a moment. "Yeah, fine, Stan. Just not feeling the greatest. Stomach's a mess. Rolaids for breakfast, you know."

"Wow, hope it's not the flu. It's going around. Have you gotten your shot?"

"No, never believed in it, Stan." Nate nodded and continued on to his office. He threw his briefcase onto the floor, then laid his head down on the desk. *Is it five yet?*

Nate struggled with his thoughts the rest of the day. "I'm no criminal," he kept telling himself, but he wasn't quite convinced. *I just have to know.*

Stan left at about 1:00 p.m. and wasn't expected back until the following day. Nate was relieved he was gone.

At about 4:00 p.m., Nate received a call, just about waking him from his desk. It was Stan with the break that Nate needed.

"Nate?"

"Stan, yeah, what's up? Everything all right?"

"Well, they ended up removing the tumor. They took one look at it and didn't need to send the biopsy to the lab, so they decided to remove it all."

"Oh, wow. Is she going to be all right?"

"Yeah, she'll need some follow-ups, but they think they got it all. She just needs rest now, which is the reason for the call. I'm probably going to be out for a while, so I need you to handle things while I'm gone."

"Got it, no problem."

"And one more thing, Nate. I have a huge, huge favor to ask. I've already tried my neighbors, and they're out of town. How are you with dogs?"

"I used to have one. Been thinking about getting another, actually."

"I need someone to watch mine for a couple of days while I'm up here with my wife."

"Consider it done, Stan. This would be a great test for Megan."

"Great! If you don't mind, there's an extra set of keys to the house in the top drawer of my desk. Could you possibly stop by my house and pick him up and keep him for a few days, until I get settled home again? Food is in the closet."

"Will do, Stan. Anything else, you just holler, all right?"

"Thanks, Nate. I owe ya one."

You owe me, all right. Nate couldn't believe his luck. Now was his chance to get the thumb drive back. He left work early and drove straight to Stan's.

The light on his gas gauge turned on as the low fuel level alarm sounded. Nate stopped at the next gas station to fill his tank. Hungry, he went inside to grab a snack to go. Beef jerky sounded good to him. After grabbing that and a fountain Coke, he was on his way.

Stan didn't live far from city hall, just a few miles past the park, and Nate was whistling Dixie. *Just a few more minutes, and all my problems are gone,* he thought. But even though he had permission, Nate still felt nervous as heck about being at his boss's house alone. He fumbled with the keys and dropped them on the front porch. The sound triggered the dog, who began barking at the top of his lungs at the side window, which was fogged up from his breath.

Nate finally opened the door and was greeted by a vicious growl.

"Holy shit!" Nate yelled. He wasn't expecting a beast. "Easy boy, easy!"

Nate stepped back outside the door, slamming it shut behind him and got on the phone to Stan.

"Stan here," he answered.

"Um, hi, Stan. It's Nate." He heard Stan laughing on the other end.

"You must have met Spike." Stan chuckled some more.

"Yeah. Spike, that's his name?"

"Sorry, I should have warned you, but you would have said no, and you didn't ask. If he doesn't hear his name in the first few seconds, he goes ballistic. He'll think you're up to no good, but he's a sweetheart. He won't hurt you as long as he doesn't suspect anything. He should warm right up to you in no time."

"Spike? Well, all right. Is he good with kids?"

"Oh yeah, he thinks all kids are innocent and wouldn't harm a hair on them. It's the adults that he watches like a shark."

"Alrighty then, sorry to bother you, Stan. Hope all is well."

"As go-d a- it gets, Nate." Stan's phone started to break up. "He – ju t a babeeee, just don't ---oss, --im--."

"Just don't what? Stan? What was that? You broke up. Stan?"

The line went dead.

"Just don't what?" Nate said to himself as he cracked the door back open. He heard a low rumble from inside. "Hey, Spike, it's me. Good boy, good Spike. That-a-boy." Nate kept talking to the dog as he pushed the door open wide. "Good boy, Spike."

The dog, a hundred-pound Rottweiler with a head the size of a beach ball, heard his name and came running to Nate, wagging his stumpy tail and wanting some affection. Nathan rubbed him all over to get him settled down and then went to work.

Where would they have that computer? he thought as he looked in all directions.

The minute he started to move, the dog let out a low growl. "Easy, Spike," Nate said. Hearing his own name calmed the dog right down again, just like Stan had said it would. Nate looked in the living room; nothing there. His search of the family room and kitchen also turned up nothing. He then made his way from bedroom to bedroom and finally came across the library, and there sat the computer, across the room on a mahogany desk. This was the only door that had been kept shut, and by the time Nate got over to the computer on the other side of the room, he realized why. *White, plush carpet. Shit,* he thought as he looked down at his shoes and over to the black shedding dog. His shoes had left a trail behind him, and straight black hair was everywhere.

He reached the desk and looked behind the computer. Sure enough, the thumb drive was still in its socket. He reached for it to yank it out, then realized it should probably be ejected first so he made his way around the desk. He didn't want any errors left on the screen. Spike started to growl again. "It's all right, Spike," he said, hoping to calm him down. It worked. Nate turned the monitor on and moved the mouse to wake the machine. Temptation started creeping in. *There's plenty of time*, he thought. He started navigating the mouse around and found Stan's documents. He clicked the mouse and pulled down to copy. Then he found his thumb-drive and right-clicked. He pulled down to paste. He thought a minute before letting go, while his conscience battled things out. The little man sitting on his right shoulder was fighting with the little man on his left.

"*Do it, man, do it. You need to know,*" said the one on the left.

"*Aw, come on, man. What are you doing? You're no criminal,*" said the other.

"*Who's the real criminal here?*" argued the left.

"*You can't use it in court anyway, buddy. Don't do it.*"

"*The satisfaction of knowing is just a click a way.*"

"*Nate, think about what you're doing. Two wrongs don't make a right, man,*" the right said.

"*But two Wrights did make an airplane, and they never would have gotten off the ground if they hadn't tried and take a few chances, buddy. Do it!*"

That was it. Nate's feuding conscience gave him all the push he needed. He released the button and the files started copying. Right away, Nate had a sinking feeling in his chest and started to shake. He felt weak in the knees and decided to sit down in the leather high-back chair. *Wow, this is nice, he* thought as he swiveled back and forth. Then he found out what Stan was trying to say on the phone before it went dead.

It must have been, whatever you do, do not sit in his chair. The dog went absolutely berserk.

"Spike! Spike! Spike! Easy, Spike! Spike, No! Easy!"

It wasn't working. Spike held him to that chair. The dog would run a lap around the library and jump back up at Nate so fast that Nate had no time to get up. He tried over and over again as Spike raced through the room, only to find himself pushed back into the chair with a hundred-pound dog on his lap, licking his face like an ice cream cone. "Easy, boy! Easy, Spike! That-a-boy. No, stop! No! Easy, Spike! Stop, please!"

It took a while, but Nate finally got Spike to settle down. He spit hair from his mouth and tried wiping the dog hair and saliva from his face, then ejected the thumb drive and pulled it from its socket. The carpet, the snow-white, plush carpet, was now embossed with tracks from Nate's shoes and the dog's feet. And everything was thickly covered with straight black dog hair and drool.

"Oh my gosh," Nate said as he looked around the room. He took a deep breath, then another. *Calm down, Nate, it will be all right.* He felt panic race through his veins like it was the Daytona 500. He tried not to hyperventilate and took more deep breaths as he scanned the room, looking at the mess. Then his eyes stopped on a cord running behind a chair. "Yes, yes," he said as he followed it to a vacuum cleaner. He went straight to work.

The vacuum was loud and scared the dog. Chaos

started all over again. The dog attacked the vacuum as if it were a villain. Spike wanted to play, jumping and snapping his jaws at it like a shark. The more he pounced, the more the hair flew. And, boy, did it fly.

Nate turned the vacuum off. "Spike! Spike, stop! Easy, Spike! No, Spike! That-a-boy." Nate took a deep breath and held it while he watched the last of the dog hair settle to the floor, and then let it go like air brakes on a bus. He guided Spike out the door and shut it. Nate leaned his back into the door as he exhaled another breath. "All right," he said as he pushed off the door to get started again.

Vacuuming took longer than expected. He also went around the room sucking up as much hair as he could find that that had landed on books, chairs, and even the desk. It was everywhere. When he finished, he placed the vacuum back in the same location and left the room, slowly backing out and closing the door.

"What in the hell is that smell?" he asked out loud as he walked down the hall and through the kitchen. The smell seemed to be everywhere he went, but he couldn't find its source. Not until he looked back to where he had already been did he realize what had happened. He saw tracks everywhere he looked. He lifted his right foot and looked at the bottom. "Hmm, nothing." Then he lifted the left, and there it was, smeared and caked into the tread. "Shit!" he yelled, and he was right. Dog shit, and it was everywhere. Everywhere the dog was not.

"Where is he? Hey, Spike," he yelled. That was mistake

number 145.

Spike was hiding, feeling bad for what he had done. But he couldn't help it. He had to go when Nate got there, and he hadn't been let out all day. All the exercise and excitement had just broken it loose. Now someone was calling his name. He was excited and came running. Spike stepped in his own shit and slid across the kitchen floor, hitting the dinette set like bowling pins. Startled, the dog got to his feet and ran like a bat out of hell through the house. Nate yelled for him to stop. When that didn't happen, he fell to his knees in surrender. "I'm dead," Nate declared. The dog whimpered back and sat gently by his side and licked his cheek. The smell was deplorable, and the mess was everywhere. Nate gave him a good scratching behind the ears and got to work.

"A bucket of hot water, some rags. I got this," Nate said, determined. He wasn't giving up now.

An hour later, Nate was loading the dog into the car, leash and food as well. He backed the car down the drive and out to the road. He was spent, but happy the car was now moving toward home. The thumb-drive was in his pocket.

"What the? You've got to be kidding me." Nate rolled down all the windows for fresh air.

When Nate got home, he let Spike roam the backyard and closed the gate. He then went in the front door, leaving his shoes on the front porch. "Hi, hon," he sighed.

"Hi, Nate. How was your day?"

"Fine, yours?" he slyly said.

Brandy heard a dog bark and looked out back. "Nate, I thought we decided that we were going to wait on getting a dog, and what the hell is that?"

"We are. That's Spike, Stan's dog. We have to watch him for a couple days while Stan's wife is in the hospital."

"Huh. One minute you're accusing him of killing our son, and the next minute you're buddies, watching his ... his beast?"

"Yeah, long story, but I thought it would be a good test for Megan."

"Yeah, maybe, but he's ... he's huge. Is he friendly?"

"Well, once he knows you. He loves to hear his name, so when he gets hyper, just call out his name, and he'll stop ... eventually."

"What about Meg? He's big enough to have her for a snack."

"Stan said he's great with kids. We'll watch him though. It will be fine."

"Well, all right."

"And, Brandy, it gave me the perfect opportunity to get this back." He held up his thumb drive. "It was still in his machine."

"Great! No more worries then. That's awesome."

Nate didn't say a word, but he sure hoped that the worries were all gone.

Nate introduced Spike to the family. He only had to call the dog's name a couple dozen times before he finally settled down. Stan was right. Spike loved kids. He and Meg got along just fine.

"What are you doing," Brandy asked Nate while he sat at the computer.

"Just checking the thumb drive. I want to see what was on it, to see if there was any info to tie it back to me."

Sure enough, there wasn't a thing on that flash drive other than Stan's folder.

"What's that folder? Nate, you didn't. Tell me you didn't."

Nate felt low, really low. He didn't know what to say. "Sorry, hon, the temptation was too great, and he'll never know."

"Never know? How can you be so sure?"

"How will he know? I have it right here, and his computer is fine. Nothing hurt."

"Boy, I hope so, Nate, or this could be really bad."

"We'll be fine, and wait until you hear everything I went through to get it."

"Hey, look how they're getting along."

Meg and Spike were playing hard together in the backyard. "Meg, come here, will you?" Nate grabbed the food and dog dishes and handed them to Megan.

"Do you know what to do with these?"

Meg grabbed them, filled one with water and the other with food, and placed them on the deck. She called Spike over. His stubby tail wagged with excitement as he ate.

•••

CHAPTER 32

Stan opened the front door to his house and pushed his wife through with their rented wheel chair a day early.

"Whoa, what is that smell?" Stan's wife said as the odor hit her like a brick wall. "Where's Spike? He always greets us at the door."

"Nathan from work has been watching Spike at his house, just until you get back on your feet. I didn't want him to spaz out and knock you over. Either our 'nose blindness' has retracted since we've been away or Spike must have gone on the floor somewhere, multiple times. He must have been excited to see someone new. I'll look around. For now, I'm getting you to bed."

After getting his wife settled in their bedroom, Stan looked throughout the house. He didn't find a thing. He cracked open a couple of windows to air the house out, then went straight to his office to check his email. Right away he sensed something different, but couldn't lay his finger on it.

He sat down in his chair behind his keyboard and clicked his screen on. He pulled a notepad out of the top drawer and started jotting down a few notes. The pen he was using had something caught in the pocket clip. It bothered Stan, so he pulled it out and had a closer look. "Hmm," a strand of dog hair. He took a closer look at his desk and found several more.

Stan shook his head, then looked down at the computer. "Hmm," he mumbled again, but this time he was nodding his head. He wasn't shocked to see that it was missing. The thumb drive that had been protruding from one of the USB slots was now gone. From the day he brought the computer home, he always wondered whose blank drive it was, Tim's or Nate's. Now he knew and his suspicions were spot on. Stan felt that he was on Nate's radar lately. He suspected it for days and only half-believed Nate's story about leaving his computer in the sunlight, the reason Nate gave for it being warm when Stan had picked it up. But Stan wasn't sure until now. "What are you looking for, my dear friend?" Stan asked himself. "You will never pin it on me, Nate. Never."

Stan finally noticed what had been bothering him since the moment he'd come into the room: the marks that the vacuum leaves in the carpet. They were fresh, and Stan had last vacuumed days ago. He chuckled. "Spike must have given him a run for his money." He looked in the vacuum, and, sure enough, it was full of white carpet fuzz mixed with a lot of straight black hair. He let out a sinister laugh.

The next day, Stan stayed home from work, as expected. His wife was doing well but not well enough to be alone. She continued to ask about the dog. She really missed Spike.

"Please?" she prodded.

"All right, dear." Stan finally gave in after the umpteenth time. "I'll go get him and bring him home today."

"Thanks so much, hon. He'll make me feel better."

The thought of the dog coming home sure put a smile on her face, but Stan wasn't smiling. He didn't know how to go about confronting Nate about snooping around in his house and in his computer. Then he also thought, *As hard as it would be, maybe I should just keep quiet about the whole thing, as if nothing happened. He didn't, after all, find anything,* Stan thought. *And acting guilty would almost be like admitting to the crime.*

Nate's phone rang. "Hello this is Nate, how can I help?"

"Nathan, Stan here. How's Spike doing?"

"Oh hi, Stan. Spike's all right. How's your wife?"

"We're home. They discharged her last night. She's doing just fine. A little sore, but she misses the dog terribly, which is strange, because she never really wanted him in the first place. But he kind of grows on you. You know?"

"Yeah, boy, does he. He's a good dog, Stan. Megan loves him."

"Is it possible I can meet you at your house at lunchtime and pick him up? It will sure lift Momma's spirits."

"You bet. Of course, Stan. Megan won't be able to say goodbye to him though. She's grown a little attached in a very short time. But maybe I can pick up a little surprise for her later. Maybe today will be the day."

"That sounds wonderful, Nate. How's 2:00 p.m. sound? Then you can take the rest of the day off. You can greet her when she gets off the bus with your surprise."

"Perfect, Stan. Thank you very much."

"No, thank you, Nate. You've been more help than you realize."

It was almost noon, and Nate had a few things to take care of before he could head out. He called Brandy to tell her the plans. She wasn't thrilled at first.

"A dog? Now? I thought we..."

"She loved having Spike visit. I think she's ready. It will be good for her."

"Well, all right, but why don't you admit it—you want a dog even more than she does."

"No denying that, hon. Listen, Stan will be there at about two o'clock to pick Spike up. I'm thinking we should take Megan to the Humane Society and have her pick one out herself. What do you say?"

"I think you're nuts, but okay. Let's do it."

Megan jumped from the bottom step of the bus to avoid a small puddle. Her mom and dad were there to greet her, as if it were her first day of school. Right away she knew something was up. She looked around but saw nothing out of the ordinary, then asked, "Where's Spike?"

A smile instantly came to Nate's face as he smirked, with an I-told-you-so look at Brandy.

"Stan came and got him and took him home, honey." Meg pouted. "Sorry, dear. I know you probably wanted to say goodbye, but we have a surprise for you." She looked up with a quizzical look. "How about we go pick out a dog of your own?" Nate looked to Brandy.

"Your own dog. You can pick him out," offered Brandy.

Megan thought for a minute and then surprised them both with a response they didn't expect. "No thanks. Not now."

Brandy's eyes got big. Nate shrugged.

"But why? I thought you wanted a dog?" Nate asked.

"Oh, I do, but after having Spike here, I see how much work and attention dogs need, and I won't have the time to train a new dog this November."

Brandy looked at Nate blankly. "What's in November, honey?"

"The NaNoWriMo competition. My teacher told me about it."

"The NaNo what?" asked Brandy.

"It's National Novel Writing Month, NaNoWriMo. See?" She spelled it out on her writing tablet.

"Okay, so?"

"Well, I'm writing a novel. Fifty-thousand words, and I'm entering." Nate and Brandy just stood there with confused looks on their faces. "It's when thousands of writers sign up to see if they can write an entire novel in thirty days. I won't have time for anything else. Between school and writing, I won't have much time for a new dog. Maybe afterward, though?" Megan smiled.

Nate and Brandy were wide-eyed and shocked that their little girl was growing up and exceeding her level of responsibility. "Alrighty then. How about this. You finish your book on time, and we will reward you with a dog of your choice from the humane society," Nate added.

Megan's smile turned upside down.

"What's wrong? I thought you'd be thrilled?" questioned Nate.

"I'll need some pencils."

•••

CHAPTER 33

"Nate, can we talk," Brandy asked.

"Sure, hon. What's up?"

"This came today. It's from the General Pencil Factory."

"Well, it's about time. They never answered my emails, and I've tried calling twice. What's it say?"

"It's says that they would love to meet Megan and that they have a surprise for her."

"Oh my gosh!" Nate and Brandy hugged for the longest time. Nate couldn't even hold back the tears. "When? When?"

"October 30th. That's almost four weeks. If we can make it."

"Oh, boy. That's about the time the trial will be getting over. Make the arrangements. Tell them we will be there, but I have to run. Court. They found a jury."

It wasn't easy to find a jury for the State versus Hernandez case, but eventually enough jurors were found. It seemed everyone in the state had heard about the school bus incident. The defense had wanted to take the trial to another county, but the judge figured that the incident had been so widely publicized, a change of venue probably wouldn't matter much. So the young man's case would be tried in his own hometown, fair or not. The jurors were sequestered. The attorneys on both sides were finally ready to continue with the case.

Some of the locals had immediately been dismissed from the pool of potential jurors for knowing the families involved, or they had kids going to the same school. The court found an equal balance of male and female jurors and even included diverse ethnic backgrounds. Even though the case seemed open-and-shut to most, the defense still had a solid case.

The judge foresaw a lot of complications with this case and estimated the trial would last three weeks, maybe longer. The citizens were confused by this estimated time.

"Three weeks? Are you kidding me? He's guilty. The kids all saw him do it," a man spoke out loud on the courthouse lawn.

"Yeah, it doesn't sound right to me either. Throw the punk in jail and throw away the key! We don't need people like that in our town. What a bully," said another bystander.

"Wait a minute, guys. He's just a kid. He may have used poor judgment, but kids fight all the time. This was just an unfortunate accident."

"Lady, if I wanted your two cents, I would have asked for it. People need to be held responsible for their actions!"

"What about the school? Should they be liable for not keeping our children safe?"

More and more folks joined in.

"Yeah, from what I understand, the bus driver was too damn fat to get down the aisle to do anything about it. Maybe he should be responsible, and him alone. I mean, really, folks, our kids are in their hands to keep them safe while they have them."

"That just gives free rein to all the bullies out there to kill whoever they want, whenever they want. That will never fly. I'm with the lady over there. You do the crime, you do the time."

More and more people joined in, drawing huge attention from passersby.

Eventually, a couple of guards showed up to break up the crowd before it got completely out of hand. But before the crowd dispersed, they realized why this case could take a while. They had only begun to cover just a few angles that were sure to be brought up during the trial.

Brandy and Nate wanted to attend the trial to show support for the family who lost their son in the horrible fight on the bus. They felt terrible, knowing that the fight started because the boy who was killed had defended Megan from a known bully. They took turns sitting in the audience as much as they could.

WEEK 1

"All rise," the bailiff barked out as the judge entered his courtroom. "Judge Joe Cockerill presides, the court is now in session. Please be seated."

The courtroom was packed, standing room only. A few people even had to be turned away. A jam-packed courtroom meant a noisy courtroom to some judges, but Judge Joe was a bit more laid-back than most and allowed the crowd to stay as long as everyone stayed quiet enough. Publicity for this trial was strong, and people came from near and far.

The courtroom wasn't only crowded the first day, but every day. People lined up in front of the courthouse early, as if they were shopping on Black Friday. One would think it was a celebrity trial, not a small town with high school kids involved. This case was important to the community. People wanted to ensure that proper justice was served.

Talk outside the courtroom remained split, some saying that kids will be kids and they will fight, while some blamed the bus driver for being too fat to fit down the aisle. A thinner driver could have made a difference and broken up the fight in time before tragedy struck. Lawsuits had been filed against the school and the driver. Some people just felt it was a very unfortunate accident and that no one was at fault. Then there were the ones who insisted that everyone take responsibility for their own actions, accidents or not, even if the future of a young man was at stake. The fact was, a life had been taken and someone had to pay, and that's what this trial was about.

Then there are some people who really wanted Carlos Hernandez to be used as an example to all bullies out there— a what-goes-around-comes-around kind of attitude. Karma. Some hoped that bullies across America would see what could happen to them when things are taken a bit too far.

Now it would be up to twelve unbiased individuals to decide which route to follow. The fate of a young man's dreams of being a professional football player was in their hands.

One witness after another was called in.

"Oh, my goodness," said Brandy, now sitting in the audience with Nate on the rare occasion that they could be there together. "They're just kids. Most of them probably would never see the inside of a courtroom, and they shouldn't have to at their age." Nate nodded as he too watched from the crowded room.

"I agree, this is terrible, but unfortunately there's no other way. They have to have witnesses," Nate replied.

"Raise your right hand and repeat after me," said the bailiff as he faced a small girl on the witness stand. The girl was shaking but complied and took a seat.

"What is your name?" The prosecutor asked.

"Cindy," the small-framed girl with blond, curly hair

answered. "Cindy Ridgecliff."

"Cindy, were you on the bus the day that this event took place?"

"Yes."

"Could you tell the court where you were sitting on the bus in relation to the incident?"

"I was sitting next to Megan, a little more than halfway back."

"Very good, Cindy. And at the time of the incident, which direction were you facing? Were you facing the front or the back of the bus?"

"Neither."

"I don't understand, there are only two options. Please explain."

"Well, I was sitting with my back against the bus wall, looking at Megan and, at times, over the seat to the back."

"I see. When you were looking back, what did you see and hear?"

"There was a lot of commotion at the time. A lot of yelling, screaming, and prodding from the kids."

"Prodding?"

"Yes. You know, encouragement."

Some members of the audience chuckled.

"So, you were saying people were applauding their actions, encouraging them to fight?"

"Yes, some were."

"Did anyone step in to try to break the fight apart?"

"Hmm. No, I didn't see anyone. Wait, yes, one boy spoke up, but then it continued."

"Was that the bus driver?"

"No, it was another football player. He told them to stop or they would get thrown off the team."

"What about the bus driver? Did he do anything?"

"He was in the front of the bus through most of it."

"Most? Please explain."

"I think he was calling for help, and when he finally made it to the back of the bus, the fighting was over."

"He did make it back there, though?"

She nodded.

"Please, audibly answer the question," the judge demanded.

"Yes, he finally made it to the back of the bus," she said.

"How long do you think it took him to get back where he was needed?"

"Oh, some time. He struggled to get past the seats."

"Can you elaborate on that a little for me, Cindy?"

She looked at him blankly. "What do you mean?"

"Well, you said, 'some time.' What does that mean?"

"Sir, you're not very educated if you don't know what 'some time' means." The courtroom erupted with laughter. Even the judge cracked a smile at that one.

"Order, let's have order in the court, please." Judge Joe smiled at the defense attorney and shrugged. "You may continue."

He took a deep breath and slowly blew the air from his cheeks, all the while reminding himself that these are kids and sometimes they will say the most off-the-wall things. He tried not to take it personally. He rubbed the back of his neck, trying to come up with a response. Instead, he restructured the question. "Do you think it took the driver two minutes to get from the front of the bus to the back, or longer?"

"Okay, since you don't know, probably longer."

He scratched the back of his head again. "Thank you, Cindy. You've been a great help."

"Can I go now?"

"Oh, one more thing, and then you can go. Do you know what started the fight?"

"Yes."

The lawyer paused for a complete answer. "Can you tell the court, please?"

"Sure. Carlos was saying some mean things about Megan and her brother. James was just trying to defend her."

"Thank you. Your witness." The attorney pointed over to the prosecutor, giving him the floor.

"Cindy, you've been a very brave girl. I just need you to be brave just a couple more minutes. Can you do that for me?"

"Sure," she nodded.

"Great. Now you mentioned the name, Carlos."

"Yes."

"Is he here in the court room today? And, if he is, can you point him out for me?"

Cindy paused for a moment, fidgeted with her hands, and played with her hair.

"It's okay, Cindy. Take your time. Just point out who Carlos is."

She took a deep breath and slowly exhaled, just as she had been taught to do when her nerves were getting the best of her. Then she raised her hand, pointing to the defendant sitting at the table in front of her. "It's him," she muttered. "He killed James."

Carlos stared Cindy down. If he showed any emotion at all, it was rage and a desire for revenge, and Cindy felt it. Her bones started to quake, stirring the marrow inside. She gasped and covered her mouth, holding back a scream. "You can step down now, Cindy. You were awesome."

Cindy slowly stood from her chair and exited the box in the front of the room, then bee-lined to her parents' side in the third row. Carlos' cold, coal eyes never left her until his eyes met her father's.

"Don't even think about it, punk," Cindy's father mouthed as his eyes burned a hole in Carlos' head.

Like telepathy in action, Carlos quickly broke his stare, and his smirk instantly morphed into a frown.

The rest of the day, and quite a few of the days that followed, were filled with kids' testimonies. Not one varied from Cindy's.

The next move by the defense attorney was an unexpected one. He scanned the audience for a brief moment, and then announced, "As my next witness, I call the principal of the school, Mr. Becktell."

"What?"

"Mr. Becktell, you are being called as a witness for the defense. Do you have any objections at this time?"

"I was never notified, Your Honor."

"We can wait another day for you to prepare, if you'd like, sir," said the judge.

"No, I have nothing to hide. Let's get this over with. I'm not sure what I can possibly add to this case, but I'm willing to help in any way I can, Your Honor."

"Very well. Please, if you would." The judge motioned the principal over to the stand. The bailiff swore him in.

"I do," the principal answered.

"Mr. Becktell, for the court, please state your full name and position at Mobley High."

"Tom Becktell, principal."

"For how many years, sir?"

"I've been there two years."

"Two years. Really? Fairly new to this, I see. And what did you do before this?"

"I was principal for thirteen years at Freedmont High in Maryland, and before that, I was dean at a boys' home."

"Oh, I stand corrected. You're quite experienced at 'principaling,' for lack of a better word." The audience chuckled out loud until they saw the judge's face, warning them to keep quiet.

"Head of administration, sir."

"Head of administration, very well. Ah, tell me more about this boys' home you were the head of."

"It was a 35,000-square-foot facility, housing some of the most troubled teens in America."

"All boys?"

"Yes, I believe I said that already."

"Troubled? Was this a prison for young boys? A juvenile home?"

"Yes."

"Yes? Which was it?"

"A very large detention center for troubled boys."

"Troubled? You mean criminal?"

"Not in all cases, but some were, yes."

"So, in this facility, you housed criminals side-by-side with bullies."

"Yes, that's pretty close."

"Weren't you afraid of the 'not quite innocent' being in danger from the guilty?"

"I object, Your Honor. What does this have to do with

this case?" the prosecutor interrupted.

The judge looked at the defense attorney. "Can we get on with this?"

"Yes, Your Honor, I'm almost there. Please, it's important. Bear with me."

The judge nodded, and the prosecutor took his seat.

The defense attorney looked over at the witness, awaiting a reply.

"I'm sorry, can you repeat the question, please?"

He looked to the stenographer for help. She read back the question, word for word. "Weren't you afraid of the 'not so innocent' being in danger from the guilty?"

"Thank you," said the defense attorney.

"The facility staff was well-trained in case of an event."

"Armed?"

"With batons and Tasers."

"Tasers. Wow, seems harsh for kids. What about guns?"

"No guns."

Judge Joe gave the defense a look, telling him to get on with it.

"Sorry, Your Honor. Just one more question and I'll be there."

"Make it quick," said Judge Joe.

The defense attorney folded his hands and breathed into them as he tried to regain his train of thought. "Compared to the bullies at your school, how would you rank the bullies at your boys' home?"

"No different, sir. Boys will be boys."

"'Boys will be boys.' That's an interesting statement."

"Your Honor?" The prosecutor jumped up from his seat.

The judge looked at the defense attorney and held up two fingers. "Two minutes."

"Mr. Becktell, *Principal* Becktell, what was the main purpose of the guards, batons, and Tasers at the boys' home."

"Well, to protect the kids, of course."

"Why? Were you responsible for them?"

"Well, of course we were."

"Then tell me, if there is no difference between those youths and the bullies at your school, why aren't the kids at your school being protected?"

Mr. Becktell fell silent.

Now it was the defense attorney's turn to look at the judge for help making the witness answer.

"Mr. Becktell, can you please answer the question," requested the judge.

"It's different, that's all."

"So you're saying that you're not responsible for the safety of the kids at your school, but you were at the boys' home?"

"That's not a fair question."

"Very well. Question withdrawn." The defense attorney

looked to the prosecutor. "Your witness."

The prosecutor stood behind his table and looked down at his watch. It was 3:45. "Your Honor, I would like to be better prepared for this witness, and it is getting late."

"Enough said. We'll continue Monday morning at 10:00 a.m. Court is now adjourned."

The people started filing out of the courtroom in an orderly manner, but as soon as they hit the doors, the press, waiting outside, went crazy.

"Tammy, from the Searchlight. Can I have a few words?" The reporter approached Jim Hernandez, the defendant's father.

"Yeah, sure. Here's a few words for you." He leaned into the mic. "You can all fuck off!" He looked up from the mic and into the young reporter's eyes. She swallowed hard, eyes wide and in disbelief that anyone would actually do such a thing. The cameraman went right over to her and wrapped an arm around her. "It's all right. It can only get better. Let's grab those people over there. They look harmless." He pointed to a couple walking down the steps, hand-in-hand. It was Brandy and Nate.

"Sir, miss? Can we have a moment?" Tammy stumbled to get the words out. "Tammy, from the Searchlight."

"Yes, of course. I love your paper, but what's with the camera?" questioned Brandy.

"Online video feeds. We'll take the stills we need from that."

"Oh, all right. Ask away."

"What do you think of the trial so far?"

"It's only been a week. It's going to be long," Nate said.

"You are?"

"I'm Nate, and this is my wife, Brandy."

Tammy jotted down their names. "Phone number, please, in case I have more questions later?"

"I'd rather not."

"Very well. Long? Why so long? I heard this was pretty much an open-and-shut case."

"Yeah, that's what we all were hoping. The defendant's lawyer is good. He's brought up things the first day that I don't think anyone even thought of."

"Things? Like what things?"

"Sorry, we really shouldn't be discussing this, not now," said Nate, pulling his wife away. "We have to run."

Brandy skipped backward, being dragged by Nate. "Sorry," she yelled back at the reporter.

"Wow, this isn't going to be easy." The reporter paused and turned. "Excuse me, Miss? Tammy, from The Searchlight. Can I have a word?"

WEEK 2

Principal Becktell took the stand again, this time with the prosecutor questioning. "Approximately how many students were enrolled at Freedmont High?"

"Roughly 1,800."

"Out of curiosity, how many of them were seniors?"

"Maybe 450 or so."

"And how many were at your boys' home?"

"I believe 6,500, all above 16 years of age. Another 1,500, age 14-16."

"Wow, really. That's quite a few. Not all locals, I hope."

"No, they were from all cultures, from just about every state."

"That has to be rough for visitors."

"It was."

"Any incidents over the years that would compare to what happened here?"

"Oh, absolutely."

"How many?"

"Over a span of 12 years, eight that I remember. A lot more minor ones."

"'Minor' meaning?"

"Small fights would break out now and then. They never amounted to much more than a few cuts and bruises, maybe a black eye or two."

"The eight incidents that you remember that were comparable, with all the weapons and guards, why weren't they stopped."

"It's just impossible to be everywhere all of the time."

"Thank you. You may step down."

"My next witness will be the manager of the bus garage," stated the prosecuting attorney.

The manager was sworn in and was ready for questioning.

"Can I have your full name, please?"

"Jackie Horn."

"Jackie, how long have you been with the garage as management?"

"Eighteen years."

"In eighteen years, you've probably seen about everything that can happen on a bus, and if not seen it, heard it?"

"Yes, there's never a dull moment."

"Anything as drastic as this over the years?"

"A couple of suicides, an overdose, and traffic accidents."

"So people have died on these buses? That's nothing new?"

"Yes, we've had deaths, but not murders."

"Objection, your honor. It has not been ruled a murder," the defense argued.

"Sustained."

"We had accidental deaths," the bus super revised her answer.

"Do you know of any regulations in the books that

specify limits to the size and weight of a driver?"

"No, sir. That would fall under 'discrimination.'"

"I see. Are there buses available to the school with wider aisles for larger people?"

"Not that I'm aware of."

"So, in your professional opinion, the buses that are in use today are up to modern standards when it comes to occupant sizes and security?"

"That is one of my jobs, to make sure everything is up-to-date. So yes, to my knowledge, everything is up-to-date and the bus was a current model."

"Thank you. Your witness, if you have further questions."

The defense attorney stood up and waved his hand. "No further questions, Your Honor."

The bus super left the stand and sat among the audience.

More kids took the stand, day after day. They were all pretty much asked the same questions, and, for the most part, gave the same answers.

WEEK 3

The estimated completion date of the trial had finally come, and the defense attorney pulled another surprise from his hat.

"For my last witness, I call Carlos Hernandez."

After a long gasp from the audience came complete

silence. Carlos was sworn in.

"Carlos. You know why we're here, and you, and only you, know exactly what happened the day of the incident. You, and only you, know what was going through your mind at the time. Please, explain to the jury what happened that day."

"Yes, I was saying things I probably shouldn't have about Megan's dead brother, and yes, James did the right thing by standing up for her and her family. Words were said, and it escalated into a brawl. I didn't mean to kill him. It was just two kids fighting." He looked over to James' family. "I know I can't bring your son back. Please, know I didn't mean to do it. It was an accident."

"Your witness."

"No questions," the prosecutor told the judge.

"Are you prepared for your final statements then?" asked the judge.

Both responded, "Yes, Your Honor."

"Proceed."

"Ladies and gentleman of the jury," the prosecutor began. "This has been a long, dragged out trial, and I'm sure that all of you are more than ready to go home to your families. Many people were blamed, and the race card was even played a time or two. This was never about the color of anyone's skin or the negligence and obesity of the bus driver. Schools have been around since the beginning of time, with policies in place to help protect the students, but we all know they can't stop the heinous acts of everyone.

"What this case was mostly about, is not just the acts of one person, but the acts of many in our community, and communities across our nation. This is about kids like Carlos who get their jollies out of hurting someone else.

"You are a witness here today. Every one of you listened while this bully outright confessed. Carlos has just admitted to every one of you that he, and he alone, started the fight, which led to the death of an innocent young man, a young man who was just standing up for what was right.

"Carlos may have regrets now, but so do most of the people sitting in prison today. It's time that we start holding people of all races responsible for what they do. Maybe, just maybe, they will think twice about their actions and reactions before tragic things, such as what happened to James, don't happen again."

"James was just being a good Samaritan, folks, and he did his best to defend someone he hardly even knew. Yet, he is gone, never to come back. His family and friends will mourn their loss the rest of their lives. And no one will ever know the man that James would have grown up to be. This world lost a patriot.

"This man who sits before you, who admitted to all of you that he started and finished this mess, cannot walk free to do it again. At the age of 16, he already has a file of misconduct a mile a long." The prosecutor took a deep breath.

"You've heard the testimony over the weeks. I only hope that you will come to the right verdict, the only verdict, and charge this man with what he deserves. Because, I'm sorry, if he walks free, that is an open invitation to every bully out there. It will tell them that it's all right to perpetrate and let things go too far. The 'it was just an accident' excuse just doesn't apply here.

"The only person who could have stopped this from happening is the same person who started it, and that person is sitting right there before your eyes. Now it's your turn to decide and bring justice where justice is deserved. Thank you all for your attendance and service to your country."

The judge looked to the defense for his closing statement.

The defense attorney rose from his chair and mockingly applauded the prosecutor for such a wonderful and terribly long speech. "That was beautiful. You, my friend, should be a speech writer." He paced the floor. "Ladies and gentleman of the jury, it has been a very long trial, and I'll do my best not to prolong it further. We all have families who we miss and would like to go home to, including this young man right here—Carlos, who had a bright football career going for him. People, kids will be kids. Things got out of hand, and a tragic accident occurred. An accident that could have been stopped by the very people who are supposed to keep our kids safe while in their care. I'm not saying what Carlos did was right. He himself is the first to admit that things went too far, but to ruin a young man's life at such an early age isn't right either.

"This, my friends, was a pure case of the failure of our school systems. They failed to have the proper procedures in place. They failed to have the right equipment. If they wanted to hire a morbidly obese man who couldn't fit down the aisle of a normal school bus, then they should have thought of the kids' safety first and purchased a bus to accommodate him. This could have been anyone's child. A child could have had a seizure or choked to death in the back of the bus before this driver could do anything about it. He's the one who should be on trial here, not Carlos. Carlos has made mistakes. We all have, as kids. Trust me when I say Carlos has learned from these mistakes." He continued.

"One child's tragic loss is enough in this accident. Let's not make it two. Acquit this young man so he can grow up and have a bright future and make a difference in this world. I thank you."

"Ladies and gentleman of the jury, the people of this state thank you for your dedicated service," the judge said. "You must now take what you have heard over the past few weeks and decide for yourselves what is fact and make your own decisions. This court is adjourned until the jury brings back a verdict."

"All rise," the bailiff requested as the judge stood up from his seat and left the courtroom.

A low murmur could be heard as the audience filed out of the room and out of the building. Once again, leaving the courthouse, they were bombarded by reporters.

"Tammy, from the Searchlight. Can I have a word from you, Miss?"

"What can I do for you?"

"Is the trial, in fact, officially over?"

"Yes, yes it is. The jury is in deliberations now."

"Do you feel good about this case? Do you think there will be a decision soon?"

"I don't feel good about this case at all. A young life was taken from this world, and another may be incarcerated, or worse, for the rest of his."

"Worse? What could be worse?" asked Tammy.

"He could be set free to do it again."

"But don't you think that after all of this, a lesson has been learned and maybe he will go on the straight and narrow?"

"Maybe. Would you be willing to take the chance and have him around your kids?"

"I see your point. Thank you for your time."

"Sir, sir, can I talk to you a minute? Tammy from the Searchlight."

It went on and on, and just not from Tammy. Reporters were everywhere. Everyone was trying to get the best sound bites, something that would boost their ratings above the rest.

"TV 5, sir. You're Jim, Carlos' father, right? How about

an interview today?"

"How about eating shit and dying," Jim rudely replied back.

"Aw, come on, sir. The people would love to hear what you have to say."

"I'm not much a of a people-pleaser. Now get that camera out of my face and move on before I wrap it around your damn neck."

"Yes, folks, that was Jim, Carlos' father. Makes you wonder where his son got his aggression from, doesn't it? Steve, Channel 5, reporting outside the courthouse."

"Can you believe that guy?" the reporter said to the cameraman.

"I certainly would hate to be involved with that family in any way. Damn."

"Look, over there." The cameraman pointed to a lone girl sitting on a bench on the courthouse lawn. She appeared to be crying. They walked over to her.

"Excuse me, Miss." She had her face in the palms of her hands. She looked up and saw the camera pointing right at her. She shied away and turned to face the other direction.

"Turn the camera off," the reporter ordered, seeing how upset the girl was. "Miss, are you all right? We're not filming. I just want to make sure you're okay."

She looked up again, her face red and her makeup smeared. "Thanks, I'm all right."

"You don't look all right. Why is this case hitting you so hard, if you don't mind me asking?"

"Carlos is going to jail, and I may never see him again."

"Oh, are you related to him?" The cameraman smirked at the reporter's question. It was clear the girl was no relation.

"No, well, kind of. We were going to get married one day."

"Oh, you're his girlfriend. I'm so sorry this has happened."

She nodded.

"You're a very pretty girl. There will be others, and besides, no one knows the outcome yet."

"I know, but..." She paused. The reporter and cameraman stood by, waiting.

"But?" The cameraman prodded her to continue.

"Everyone will think he's a bad person, regardless."

The cameraman sat next to her and wrapped his arm around her, but she winced when he touched her arm. The reporter looked down and noticed a very large bruise on the girl's arm. "Oh, wow, are you all right? That's quite a bruise."

The cameraman then motioned to the reporter to look at the girl's face. Looking closer, they could easily see where her tears had washed away the makeup that had been covering an old black eye. The swelling was gone, but the color remained, though faded.

"Who did this to you?" asked the cameraman.

"I fell."

"You fell, my ass. I had my share of fights growing up in the hood. I know what a week-old shiner looks like. Carlos did this, didn't he?" She didn't answer, but they knew.

"What are you doing with a guy who treats you that way, Miss?"

"He can be a real nice guy when he wants to," she finally said.

"And when he doesn't want to?" She shied away again. "Did you make a police report?" He waited for an answer, but none came. She clammed up. "Well, you're making one now." The cameraman pulled his cell phone from his pocket and dialed 911. The police arrived within minutes and convinced the girl it was the right thing to do. "He's just going to do it again," an officer told her. "If not to you, to someone else."

The jury had deliberated for hours into the night, the next morning, and into the following days. No one knew what to think. The jury could be out a week or have their decision tomorrow.

"What's your gut feeling on the case, Nate?" asked Brandy as they lay in bed, staring at the ceiling.

"I really don't know, hon. The defense was strong all the way to the end."

"Could you believe that speech the prosecutor made?"

"Yes, wasn't that awesome?"

"Yes, I just hope it didn't backfire on him, being so long and all."

"The only thing we know for sure is that we know nothing for sure."

"Boy, isn't that the truth. Goodnight."

"Goodnight, dear."

●●●

CHAPTER 34

"I can't believe this day finally came," said Brandy.

"Yeah, I know, right? You excited back there?"

"Sure am, Dad!" Megan replied.

"And, with any luck, the jury will be in deliberation for one more day so we can be there for the verdict too. That's going to be ugly."

"Look!" Brandy pointed.

"Yeah, there it is," Nathan said as he drove into town.

"Where? Where?" questioned Megan excitedly.

"Over there." Nate pointed to a very large factory, which came into view as he pulled the car into the parking lot.

"Wow look at this place. It's huge," Brandy added. "And old."

The factory was an old brick-and-mortar building, which resembled an old, run-down car-assembly plant from back in the 1940s or 50s. Nate negotiated his way across the parking lot, dodging countless potholes like a football player avoiding a tackle. The car rocked back and forth and, on occasion, up and down as some of the potholes were unavoidable.

"I guess we are about a week early," Nate said.

"Why is that, dear?" Brandy asked as she braced herself for another imminent hit.

Nate nodded in the direction of some trucks parked on the other side of the lot. They all bore the logo of an asphalt company and looked as if they were about to start repaving the lot.

Brandy nodded as her head slammed into the roof of the car. The car's shocks bottomed out with a loud bang.

"Dammit!" she yelled.

Nathan negotiated one more turn before parking the car in the guest parking spot next to the empty employee-of-the-month space. "Maybe he's out to lunch?" Nate shrugged, looking back at Brandy.

Brandy looked at her watch. It was 9:05 a.m.; they were five minutes late. She shook her head with disgusted look, then practically landed on her behind at the same time. She'd stumbled when her heel dug deep into the broken pavement. The asphalt was in desperate need of repair.

She walked off the pain in her ankle as it began to throb. She then grabbed hold of Megan's hand, wondering if this was a mistake. Nate grabbed Megan's other hand, creating a human swing as they swung Megan between them, over each crater in the pavement on the way to the front door.

The door chimed as they walked between two freshly painted ten-foot-tall number-two pencils, standing guard on either side of the door.

"May I help you?" the receptionist said, readily popping her head up from her computer screen.

"Yes, the CEO is expecting us," Nate answered with confidence while adjusting his tie. "Can you please tell him we're here?"

"Sure, your name?"

Nate looked around the room somewhat disappointedly. He'd expected more. He cleared his throat. "Just tell him that Megan is here and is very excited to meet him."

"Very well." She grabbed the receiver and dialed the phone.

"David here," a voice on the other end answered.

"Mr. Woodall, I have a very excited little girl in the lobby here to see you."

"It must be Megan. I'll be right down."

The receptionist hung up the phone. "You folks can have a seat over in the lobby while you wait. There's coffee and soft drinks." She nodded in the direction of the lobby.

Brandy offered thanks, with a slight curtsy.

"What was that?" Nate asked, almost chuckling at the awkwardness.

Brandy slapped his shoulder. "I'm nervous, all right? I was just trying to be polite."

"Just be yourself, dear. You'll be fine," he replied. He had never seen her curtsy before and obviously never wanted to again.

They made their way over to the refreshments. The fountain taps resembled the tops of pencils with erasers, all with handwritten labels. Everyone grabbed their favorite drink and waited. Nate, with a slight interest in architecture, scanned the room, thinking that the building was an architectural nightmare. *A mixture of late 40s and early 50s, mixed with pencil,* he thought. Minutes passed and Megan was getting antsy.

"Should be anytime, dear. Please settle down," Brandy said. "Look, there is a drawing table with all kinds of pencils over there. Why don't you draw something for the CEO while we wait?"

Megan looked at the drawing table and then looked to the sketchpad she was carrying in her backpack. "But I already did," she replied.

Just then, they heard a loud bang, and just to their right, a pair of large stainless steel doors swung open. A man on a modified golf cart drove through. The sides of the cart resembled large pencils with the eraser end protruding from the front of the cart, acting as bumpers.

"David?" Nate questioned.

"You must be, Nate." Nate nodded. "Brandy?" Dave bowed, grabbing her hand for a kiss. Brandy peered at Nate as David bowed, thinking her curtsy wasn't as out of place as Nate had made it out to be. Dave then turned toward Megan. "And you," he said. "Don't tell me, let me think." He looked to the ceiling, rattling off a few names to himself as he thought. "You must be Megan," he finally said, bowing before her, hands clapped together.

Megan smiled wide, excited that he remembered her name.

"Hello," she said meekly.

"First, I must apologize to all of you for the runaround you got on the phone and email when you first tried to contact us," David said as his gaze ping-ponged back and forth from Brandy to Nate. "Please understand, we get bombarded with calls every day from people who want to see how a pencil is made. We are just now getting set up for such tours, but as you can see, we have a long way to go. The parking lot is a week behind, and, well, we're getting there on the inside. We understand that it could be very educational for schools and would like to be a part of that one day. Soon, hopefully. Until I received Megan's letter, we had no idea just how important this was. Well, here we are."

"Letter?" Brandy asked. "I didn't know." Nate and Brandy both looked down at Megan, Brandy giving her half of a hug.

"Are you folks ready?" asked David.

They nodded.

"Well then, climb aboard. Let me give you the first official General Pencil Factory tour." David motioned to the pencil cart.

They weren't expecting this. Now all three were equally excited. They all boarded the cart.

"Seatbelts, please. Safety, rather than sorry," Dave said as he looked over his shoulder to make sure everyone was buckled in. "Megan, please sit here in the front, next to me." Dave patted the front passenger seat with his hand.

Megan looked to her dad for approval. Nate nodded, "Absolutely, go on," he said.

David checked once again for seatbelts and then set the cart in motion. They barely got moving when Dave slammed on the brakes, throwing everyone forward. Brandy yelled.

"I'm so sorry! Are you all right?" David inquired.

"Yeah, I'm fine." Brandy sat back up in her seat and straightened her skirt.

David couldn't help but to sneak a peek in the rearview mirror, eyebrows raised. "I almost forgot," he said, grabbing a clipboard and a pen from the dash. "Would you all please sign on the bottom?"

"What's this?" Nate asked.

"Just standard procedures, I promise. Insurance requires it so we aren't responsible for any accidents. You understand, right?"

Nate looked at Brandy, the brains of the family.

"We don't have to do this, you know," Dave added, feeling a breeze of hesitation in the air.

"Dad, please," Megan whined from the front seat. Brandy grabbed the clipboard from Nate's hands and signed at the bottom. She then shoved it back in Nate's gut and prodded him to sign as well.

"Well, all right. This pencil mobile can't go very fast anyway," Nate joked while Dave watched the pen dance across the signature line.

"Just 0-50 in 14 seconds. We race them on a track out back, after shifts," Dave said as he reached for the clipboard. It took a moment for him to realize what he had just said. "But I personally never drive it over 15 miles per hour." Nate reluctantly handed him the clipboard.

Dave quickly looked the document over, ripped the bottom sheet out and returned it to Nate. "Shall we?" he asked, right before he set the cart into motion again. The cart spun its tires on the slippery floor before taking off. A high-pitched squeal echoed through the room. Dave looked over his shoulder to Nate. "Just playing," he joked. His smirk slowly faded from his face.

The cart quickly moved across the floor toward two very large, dark-grey doors, almost the color of graphite. "Hold on, little bump," Dave warned. The door wasn't opening, and they weren't slowing. Brandy braced for impact while Nate reached for Megan.

"David, watch out! You..." Nate yelled right before the electric cart hit the doors with a very soft thump. The erasers at the front end of the cart absorbed 99.9% of the impact. The doors, which looked as if they weighed 500 pounds each, freely swung open wide, allowing for the cart to pass straight through.

"Whoa, what was that all about?" Nate asked. Megan giggled from the bottom of her belly in the front seat. That's something they hadn't heard in a long time.

"Nate, Brandy. I admit this tour is all new to me, but I assure you that it's perfectly s—"

Nate and Brandy held each other as they stared at their daughter in the front seat, giggling her heart out. They were paying no attention to what David had just said. It'd been such a long time since they'd heard their little girl laugh like that. They just sat back and took it all in. Brandy sighed.

David realized they were caught up in a moment that he could not compete with, so he gave them as much time as they needed before moving on with the tour.

Moments later, Megan stopped laughing, and David set the cart back in motion. "Okay, folks, we just left the lobby and now we are in the foundry, where we make the pencil leads." Dave looked at Megan. "But, there's no lead in a pencil, is there, Megan?" Megan shrugged and looked back at her mom and dad for help. Brandy shrugged as well and shook her head no, guessing. "No, of course not. Lead is poisonous. Lead has not been used for writing utensils since the Romans and Egyptians used it in their writing styluses. Wooden pencils never had it and never will. The lead is just a name we use for our mixture of clay and graphite."

David pointed to some large vats. "The graphite powder is mixed with clay in those over there. It's mixed for hours to just the right texture, then made into cakes and left to dry." Megan smiled at the mention of the word 'cake' and rubbed her tummy. "Sorry, Megan, wrong kind of cake. The cakes are then stuffed into a press, right over there," he pointed in another direction, "where they are then pushed through tiny holes, like a Play-Doh machine." Megan smiled again, thinking of when she played with her Play-Doh at home. She used to play with it all the time. "This forms the rod like leads. Then they are washed and dried and fired in a large oven, then washed and dried again." David looked over his shoulder and saw that he was losing Megan. *Oh, the attention span of a seven-year-old,* he thought.

"Next stop is our wood shop." The cart moved forward toward another pair of steel doors. This perked Meg's attention up a little, as she sat and wondered if they were going to crash through that door as well. David continued reading from his notes on the clipboard. "Most of our pencils are made from cedar. The wood is soft, easy to cut, and has nice linear grain to work with. Grooves are cut into the planks, and inside the grooves are where we lay the lead. The two planks are then glued together, sandwiching the lead inside."

"Excuse me, Dave?" Nate interrupted. "You said they make the pencils from cedar?"

"Yes, that's right, mostly."

"But our tree was a maple."

"Yes, yes it was. That means it was a special order for a client and manufactured in the specialty warehouse. It's set up for shorter runs for harder woods. The presses couldn't run nearly as fast or they would burn up, and no one likes the smell of charred pencils." Dave turned to Megan with a pencil mustache for a laugh. She giggled. "Maple pencils also are harder to sharpen in pencil sharpeners." He shook his head. "I'm sorry, I digress. Let's move on, shall we?" Dave turned the cart down a narrow path. "The pencils are then carted over to the next room, where they are painted and fitted with a metal jacket and eraser. After that they go over there to the right and get embossed with a logo and name, and are then foil-stamped. Not necessarily in that order. Or is it?" he questioned, drawing arrows on his clipboard. "Ah, and yes, that is where the heart, your heart, Megan—the one you drew and carved into Ash—were embossed onto the pencils, as well." David handed Megan one of her special pencils. Her smile couldn't have gotten any bigger.

"So you're saying that someone special-ordered those pencils?" asked Nate.

"Yes, it was a small run of about 20,000 pencils for a writing organization in Colorado. "Write with your Heart" was their slogan. They really only wanted 12,000. Minor error on our part, so we sold the rest to a nationwide chain store. My nephew worked here at the time and made all of the arrangements. He's off to college now. I suspect he'll return in the summer. Anyway, it all worked out. We're coming up to your bins next."

The cart traveled for what seemed like miles through warehouse and machine shops, and every little thing was shown in great detail, all the way down to the process of crimping the band around the pencil and eraser. Megan learned all about all different kinds of pencils. She never realized just how many there were. There was a pencil for every imaginable task—large ones for carpenters to hold, and drawing pencils with a variety of leads depending on how dark of a line the artist needs to draw, right down to the most popular pencil used in every office and school in the world. The number-two pencil.

The cart motored past a series of archways with small signs above each, which read, "Testing 1," "Testing 2," and so on, all the way up to "Testing 12."

"What are those?" Megan asked.

"Oh, those. I almost forgot. Every pencil here at General Pencil goes through some very rigorous testing before receiving our stamp of approval. Those are the rooms where the testing is done."

"Can we look?"

"Look? Oh, that's really not on the tour. That's very confidential stuff."

"Please? We won't tell." Meg looked back at her mom and dad.

"Megan, it's not on the tour, honey. Let's just go look at what we came here for." Megan's eyes filled with sorrow, a look all too familiar to the family.

"Well, all right," David said. "We'll take a peek in a couple of the rooms, but we must be quiet. The kids who work here love their jobs but hate to be disturbed."

A smile returned to Megan's face as the cart came to a rolling stop a short distance from the archways. Dave lifted the rope holding a sign that read, "Deaf/Handicap Area, proceed with caution." This puzzled Megan and her family.

"Kids?" Nate asked.

"Shh. That's right, kids. We must walk from here," Dave whispered as the family ducked under the rope. "We must be very quiet."

"But…"

"All in good time," Dave interrupted.

They slowly approached the first room. There was no door, just an archway. They peeked around the corner. Megan was mesmerized. "Children?" she too questioned.

"Shh. Yes, Megan, children, except some aren't that young. But they are all young at heart."

"What do you mean?" Brandy whispered.

"They're considered 'Dawn's Kids.' We have one of the largest populations of these kids in our area, and they all needed a place to go. I brought them here."

"Special needs?" asked Brandy.

"Yes, they have unique symptoms of Down syndrome and more. Dawn was the first who showed signs of being different. Then they just started coming out of the woodwork. They all share common traits, besides full-blown Down syndrome. They all have cleft palate. Some have severe learning disabilities, and none have survived past the age of 33."

"Autism?" questioned Brandy.

"Maybe one form or another, but, in my opinion, they were wrongly diagnosed and forgotten about. Dawn's kids are also usually social butterflies, but not these kids. These kids are different in so many ways. They like it here."

"What is he doing?" Megan asked pointing to one of the kids who looked like a 12-year-old boy but was actually 23. He was moving a pencil between his fingers at a very rapid rate. He had one pencil going in each hand, looping them in between each finger and then back again. The pencils were moving so fast that they appeared as if they were in sync with each other.

"That's Bobbie. He's testing the pencils for balance. He's very good. If he drops one, there's probably something wrong with the lead or the density of the wood. Our pencils are perfectly balanced, and he hardly ever drops them, but when he does, we stop the presses and find the problem." Nate looked at Dave as if he were pulling his leg. "It's true.

Come on, before he sees us." Dave motioned them on.

They moved to the next doorway and peeked around the corner so they wouldn't disturb anyone. Inside was a little boy who appeared to be about eight years old. He was sitting at a drum set in the middle of the room. He started drumming to the music that was playing, but he was using pencils as drumsticks.

"That's Curwood. He also tests for balance but goes one step further. He tests for durability too." Nate looked at Dave again, as if he'd lost his mind, and listened to the beat Curwood was pounding out. "All our pencils are built tough and designed to take a fall without breaking the lead. If one breaks, Curwood, of course, will let us know."

They continued on, room after room. In the next room, a little boy had a pencil pinched between his upper lip and nose, while another pencil was pinched between his fingers, and he was giving his best Groucho Marx impression in front of a mirror. Nate looked at Dave, eyebrows raised, awaiting an answer to his unspoken question.

David answered, "Character, Nate, and thickness. Too thick, he'll know and the pencil will drop to the floor. His lip curl is one size, and one size only." Dave shrugged then moved to the next doorway.

Room number four was much bigger than the rest and was more like what they had expected to see in a product-testing area. Here, several drawing tables were set up across the room. The tables were labeled, 2B, H, HB, H2, H3, H4,

H5, and so on. At each station was a kid scribbling on the paper taped to the table. They were testing the hardness of the leads and comparing them to the chart in front of them. No dumb look came from Nate this time, but Dave checked for his approval anyway. Nate just smiled back.

The next room contained a couple of drawing tables as well. "This is our resident artist, Aaron. He does beautiful work. His drawings are superb, and if a pencil fails his inspection, he lets me know immediately. He's also the one who got great vibes from the pencils made from your tree and noticed the heart carved in it. He drew several pictures of it and made a cast for the embossment in your pencil. He, and he alone, is responsible for preserving Ash.

"I'll be right back," David said as he walked toward Aaron. He whispered in Aaron's ear, right before he looked over his shoulder at Megan. Megan ducked away. Aaron shook his head, and Dave returned to the group.

"On to the next room," David said. They peeked around that corner as well. Immediately, Nate started to laugh. "Let me guess, David. Elasticity?"

"You're absolutely correct, Nate," Dave answered. Inside was a young girl holding a pencil between her forefinger and thumb. She was moving her hand up and down in front of her face. The pencil appeared to bend right before her eyes. If it didn't, there was something wrong.

"Well that's about it," David said.

"What about the rest of the rooms?" asked Megan.

"They're more of the same, Megan, except they are part of our colored-pencil division. Brand new and extremely confidential, as our main competitor is unaware of us hitting that market."

As they returned to the cart, a siren blared and lights flash above doorway number two. Curwood's room. "Uh-oh," said David. "Curwood must have dropped one."

Within seconds, silence fell. The presses had stopped running, and three workers had entered Curwood's room.

"Wow, that's faster than our local fire department," mentioned Nate.

"We take their work very seriously. If we don't respond quickly, thousands of flawed pencils will be made, and we can't have that now, can we?"

Nate still couldn't believe what he'd seen and was waiting for John Quinones to come out with his mic and cameras. Instead, they moved on to what had brought them to the factory in the first place. The cart moved forward and bumped into the next set of steel doors, labeled, "Special Projects."

"Ahh, here we are, Megan. Your tree came to us by mistake, actually. A guy in a city truck said he had a tree for sale and wanted to know if we were interested. When we found out what it was, we told him no, that we were only accepting cedar at this time. That's when our own resident artist, Aaron, came walking in from lunch. All he did was talk about the energy he felt as he passed by the tree in the parking lot. It was he who found the heart you carved in it. He told me then that it was a special tree, so we brought it in and prepped it.

Funny thing is, we received a special order the very next day that utilized that exact tree. The order was perfect for your tree, which is why all of those pencils were branded with your heart."

"Well, it's good to know that it went to a good organization," said Brandy, as she wiped tears from her cheeks.

"Your pencils were made right over there." David pointed and drove the cart toward a large bin near the wall. "But I'm afraid we don't have many of those pencils left. We are happy to give you the proof pulls of the run, though. You see. Every 50th pencil is pulled and tested for quality, and if it's fine, they continue the press. If not, the presses are stopped and adjusted. The bad pencils get tossed out. The good pulls go in this bin right here. Megan, you are welcome to as many as you want. All, if you like."

Nate picked Megan up so she could see over the edge of the bin. Her eyes couldn't have gotten any brighter. She couldn't believe just how many pencils there were. She was in Heaven.

"There's hundreds of them," said Nate. "More than enough for a lifetime, Megan."

"I can finish my book," Megan said as she turned and smiled. "NaNoWriMo!"

"All of them." Nate confirmed.

"All of them," Dave said.

Brandy started to cry. Nate was having trouble holding back his tears himself.

They quickly boxed up the pencils and headed back to the lobby, where they would say their goodbyes. The tour was over, and it was time to leave.

"Well, I hope you enjoyed the tour," Dave offered.

"Boy, did we. We can't thank you enough," said Brandy, still teary-eyed.

"When I received your daughter's letter explaining all that happened, I could hardly refuse. It was such a fascinating story, and I'm more than happy to do it." He turned to Megan. "I hope these pencils inspire you to write that perfect novel one day."

Megan smiled and pulled a drawing from her sketchbook. "I drew this with one of your pencils. It's Ash. It's for you," Meg said, handing the drawing over to Dave.

"Oh, my. This is beautiful. Thank you." Dave bent down and gave Megan a kiss on the cheek.

"We have a few gifts for your family, as well, for coming down. Dave handed each of them a large inflatable pencil, a tee shirt with the company logo, and a pair of matching coffee mugs for Brandy and Nate. "Oh, I almost forgot. We have one more very special gift for this talented young lady." Just then, Aaron carried a long box over and handed it to Dave. It looked like a box of long-stemmed roses.

"During every special project that we do, we pull a branch from the tree, and one of our artisans carves it into a large pencil, which gets hung on the wall. It's just something that we do. Open it."

Megan looked to her dad for help. "Pull the ribbon, honey." She pulled. Nate lifted the top. Inside lay a large beautifully carved pencil with a lanyard. Engraved on it was an exact replica of the heart that Megan had carved in the tree. There wasn't a dry eye in the lobby.

Nathan shook David's hand once again, thanking him over and over. Brandy hugged Dave's neck and kissed him on the cheek multiple times.

They said their goodbyes, loaded up the car, and headed for home.

It was another silent ride home, Megan in the back seat testing out the pencils she'd received, drumming them against her sketchpad and making them bend to test their elasticity. Nate chuckled when he saw her best impression of Groucho Marx in the rearview mirror. Everyone was in complete awe of the day.

Halfway home, Nate turned the radio on to see if there was any news about the trial.

"There was a shooting today at the local courthouse, shortly after the verdict was read to the general audience just outside..."

"What? No!"

•••

CHAPTER 35

The news report paused for a commercial break.

"Come on, come on!" Nate impatiently waited for the news to resume, while driving home from the biggest day of his daughter's life. "Come on! Who shot who?"

"That's right folks, you heard it here first. Shortly after a guilty verdict was read, chaos broke loose on the courtyard's front lawn. First, there were arguments, and your expected protests, but then, all of a sudden, someone started yelling a name, and bullets started to fly.

"Reports from the scene indicate that several people are injured, and two are dead, one being the shooter, Carlos' father, Jim. This just happened moments ago. Details are still sketchy, but we'll keep you informed here on WCRK, FM97.1."

"Oh, my gosh!" Brandy said, her hand covering her mouth.

Nate stared out the car's windshield, mouth agape, speechless. He grabbed his phone but didn't even know whom to call. Lucky for him, he didn't have to call anyone. His phone rang.

"Hello, this is Nate."

"Nate, thank God you're all right."

"Stan?"

"Yeah, are you down there?"

"No, Stan, we couldn't go."

"Good or you would probably be dead. He was looking for you, Nate. He fired some shots. He killed a guard, then turned the gun on himself. Glad you're all right."

"Are you all right, Stan? You don't sound well."

"I'll be fine, Nate. Took one in the shoulder. Headed to the hospital now. Got to go, Nate."

"Thanks, Stan. Thanks for..." The line went dead. "… calling."

"Everything all right?" Brandy asked.

That was Stan. He's been shot. He said Jim was calling out my name. He was looking for me. He was going to kill me." Nate pulled the car off the road to catch his breath. "I guess it's a good thing we didn't go. Ash saved my life."

•••

CHAPTER 36

"It's been quite a ride, Nate."

"Yes, it has, dear."

"So glad that trial's over."

"Yeah, me too. It appears the bus driver is going to get his job back, as well. I hear they are customizing a bus just for him to drive."

"Yeah, that's great! And look at what happened to Stan. Karma sucks."

"Sure does. You know, why don't you close the Kickstarter down when we get home. I just don't have the energy to pursue it anymore. And besides, it won't bring Ash back. We know who did it, and I think Karma is taking care of that for us."

"Will do. I feel the same way. Where do we go from here?"

"We just keep moving forward."

"Do you think she'll be all right?"

"Megan? She'll be fine. I don't think we have to worry about any of that cutting nonsense ever again, either. She has enough pencils to last a lifetime, and her brother's spirit will be right there with her."

"Just look at her, Nate. She sure is getting big."

"Yeah, she sure is." Nate smiled.

Brandy and Nate were walking hand-in-hand on a nature trail in the same park where Nate practically lived for three weeks. As they walked around the pond, Megan sat on a picnic table under some trees, writing in her journal and drawing pictures—doing what she loved.

"She looks so happy now," Brandy said. "Great to see that she has her spark back, isn't it? What do you think she's working on?"

"I've asked many times, but she won't budge. Not sure what the big secret is. I just give her the space she needs to create."

They strolled another time around the pond, always keeping a close eye on their daughter. They only stopped for a brief moment to watch a frog, half submerged in the duckweed, as a mute swan gracefully swam by. Brandy glanced over to check on Meg.

She grabbed Nate's arm. "Where's Meg?"

The picnic table was empty. Only her journal and sketchpad remained, pages blowing in the breeze.

"She's right over... She's gone," Nate said.

They scanned the area, but she was nowhere to be seen. Brandy started to panic, quickly followed by Nate. Then the yelling began. "Megan?"

"Megan!" Brandy yelled.

Nate started picking up the pace as he looked around for their daughter. Brandy caught up, and then they were off at a full-fledged sprint, both yelling at the top of their lungs.

Brandy did her best to keep up but lagged behind, looking in another direction as she ran. Then she saw her. "Megan! Nate, over there!" She pointed to the left under some trees in the distance.

Nate breathed a sigh of relief. They stopped in their tracks and looked on, panting like dogs. "What do you think she's doing?"

"Well, I don't know. She sure is looking closely at the trees. Do you think she's looking for tree spirits?"

"Wow, I didn't think of that. She's talking to someone, though. Come on."

"There's no one over there. Not that we can see, anyway. Maybe someone is hiding behind that big tree."

"Or maybe up in the tree," Nate added as he noticed Meg peering upward at the trunk.

Megan was looking up and down, looking at all of the long branches. She examined the bark and felt the roughness with her palms and fingertips. Nate and Brandy where close enough now that they could hear a noise. A barking sound was coming from high above. Looking closer, they spotted a squirrel looking down at Megan. It was barking like a little dog. Just to the right of it was a hole in the tree with three tiny heads peeking out. The squirrel was just warning its young of possible danger. Little did it know that Megan would never hurt them. Before Nate and Brandy could get there, Megan had already moved on to another tree.

Megan looked that tree over, as well. Nate swore that he saw her talking to that one too.

"What did they say, Megan?" Nate asked as they approached.

"What did who say, Dad?"

"The trees. We saw you talking to them. Did they talk back?"

"Are you feeling all right, Pop?"

"Yeah, I feel fine, Megan. Why do you ask?"

"Because you're being silly. You know that trees don't talk." She turned to the closest tree and whispered, "I have to go. Goodbye." She looked back at her mom and dad and giggled. She then turned and walked back to the bench where she had left her sketchpad and journal. She hummed a tune as she walked. "Like a Tattoo," again, by Jordin Sparks.

Nate and Brandy looked at each other and shrugged.

"Our daughter has officially become a smartass."

"Nate!" Brandy was shocked.

"Everything is going to be all right."

"Yes it is, Nate. Yes it is."

•••

CHAPTER 37

Fall and winter came and went, with an early spring being a welcome surprise. The whole family was out working in the backyard. Brandy was in the flowerbeds, weeding. Megan was sitting on Ash's tree stump, working hard on the edits to her story, while Nate mowed the lawn.

With each pass with the mower, Nate would look over and smile at Meg. She still looked sad at times, missing Ash, for sure. Nate wished there was something more he could do.

About the fifteenth time around the yard, Nate noticed Megan was no longer writing. Instead, she seemed to be mesmerized by a raven that had just landed on the roof of the house. It appeared to be interested in something in the eavestrough. It dug around a little, took one look at Megan, and with a nod, went on his way.

Every day, the large black bird showed up on the roof and did the same thing. Nate assumed that the bird had found a food source—maybe some grubs or worms—and, admittedly, the eaves were in desperate need of cleaning. With everything that had happened in the previous year, that was one project, among many, that had not been addressed.

Nate decided today was going to be the day he'd tackle that chore. It was a task he never looked forward to, but it had to be done. When he went out to the shed to grab a ladder and a pail, he noticed the raven take off from the roof again.

Well, my friend, I hope you find another food source soon. This one will be gone today, he thought as he carried the ladder from the shed to the house.

Nate climbed up the ladder, not too far from where the raven always sat, and set the bucket down on the roof. He pulled some garden gloves from his back pocket and put them on. From the corner of his eye, he noticed the raven, watching him from high up in a nearby tree. "Sorry, buddy, it's got to be done," he said as he reached in for the first scoop of muck from the trough.

Going back for more, Nate hesitated when the raven let out a loud screech and a couple of clucks. Nate looked back at the bird. It was shaking its head wildly. "I'm sorry, fella. I don't like it either, but it has to be cleaned out."

The bird didn't stop. He carried on with all of the noises that ravens make. Then he started to dance and bobbed his head up and down with excitement. With all of the raven's racket, Nate became curious. He looked down inside the eave, expecting to see grubs and worms, but he saw nothing out of the ordinary. Then he looked a little to the left, and there it was. The greenery that had overtaken the rest of the gutter was neatly groomed away so that it would get plenty of sunlight and nourishment. It stood proud and tall, well, as tall and as proud as a maple tree sapling could be.

Nate just stared at the little tree in wonder. *"Ash?"*

"Brandy! Megan! Come here, quick! You have to see this." Nate yelled.

• The End •

AFTERWORD

ASH, Like a Tattoo — The novel.

My name is Megan Renard, and this was my story about my big brother, Ashton, whom I never was privileged to meet in person. Thank you for taking the time to read my book, a story that I wrote during the 2013 NaNoWriMo under the pen name of Dan Waltz.

ASH, Like a Tattoo
Bullycidal Behavior

by Dan Waltz

(alias, Megan Renard)

www.bullycidal.com

ABOUT THE AUTHOR

Dan Waltz:

> *Dan's artwork tells their own stories,*
> *and his stories paint their own pictures.*

Dan's love for nature shines through with every finely tuned brushstroke of his realistic wildlife paintings. His drawings and paintings have graced the covers and insides of many national catalogs, novels, and kids' books across America. His written words have spoken to kids and adults alike, in both paperback and ebook formats, and have sold thousands around the globe. His love for horror, fantasy, and drama is reflected in every written word, with detailed stories that usually take on double meanings and rarely end the way you think they will. Filled with twists and turns, Dan's stories aim to keep you intrigued from start to finish.

Visit Dan online at www.danwaltz.com, and follow him on all major social media networks.

> *"Every day starts with a blank canvas. What picture will you paint for all to see today?"* ~ DW

www.danwaltz.com

Book Club Discussion Questions
ASH, Like a Tattoo by Dan Waltz

1. Knowing the circumstances: What did you think when Nathan didn't tell Brandy that he'd lost his job that day? Do you think he did the right thing? What would you have done?
2. Have you ever been bullied or know anyone who has been bullied?
3. Do you think bullying starts at home, or is it learned from peers?
4. Do you think bullying is the same today, or has it gotten worse since you were in school?
5. What would you recommend to someone who is being bullied? (* Notice "do nothing" isn't an answer.)
    A. Stand up for yourself.
    B. Tell someone.
    C. Talk to them and encourage them.
    D. Get them help.
    E. If he or she is young, tell their parents.
    F. All of the above.
6. Does a biodegradable urn sound like a good idea to you? Would you ever consider one? If so, where would you bury/plant it? Your yard? Park? Woods?
7. What did you think of the pencil factory tour, and what did it most remind you of, and why?
8. Have you ever been to a psychic of any kind? (fortuneteller, tarot reader, palm reader, etc.) Did you go for fun? Would you go for advice like Brandy did? Would you ever take the advice seriously? Or do you think they are all fakes?
9. What would you do if you thought your boss betrayed you?
    A. Call him out.
    B. Try to gather enough evidence to prove it like Nate did.

C. Look for a NEW job.

D. Try to look past it for the sake of your job.

10. Do you think the Mayor got what he deserved? (Karma)

11. What do you think ever happened to the Mayor?

12. Who was your favorite character, and why?

13. Who do you think the hero in the story was, and why? (No correct answer)

14. Who would you recommend ASH to?
    1. Schools
    2. Teens
    3. Adults
    4. Anyone

15. Do you think Mac, the bus driver, was at fault for the outcome of the fight? What about the school?

16. What did you think of the school counselor?

17. Your thoughts on Mayor Sam?

18. Over all, what did you think of ASH: Like a Tattoo?

19. What did you think of the ending? Predictable?

20. What genre best suits ASH: Like a Tattoo and why?
    1. Fantasy
    2. Horror
    3. Drama
    4. Family

21. What would you think if a face suddenly appeared on a tree in your yard?
    1. Do a double take and think of ASH.
    2. Think nothing of it.
    3. Take a photo of it and post it to Dan Waltz's Facebook wall.

22. What do you think happened to the Mayor?
    A. Won his re-election.
    B. Resigned from office.
    C. Admitted his wrongdoing and apologized.
    D. Died due to complications on the operating table.

If you enjoyed ASH, Like a Tattoo
please let the author know by leaving a review on
Amazon and Goodreads and share it with your friends.
It will be greatly appreciated.

Spread the word and help stop bullying!

Titles by Dan Waltz

- Kornstalkers, Corn Maze Massacre
- Dragon • Fly, A Gnomes Great Adventure
- Endangered Domain (Short Story)
- Viral Bound (Zombie Novel)
- Ash, Like a Tattoo: Bullycidal Behavior

Titles in the works:

- Field of Screams
- Carnyville
- Memorial Highway
- 2026
- Graffiti Artist
- and more…

Follow Dan on all the major social media networks.